Sleeping Dogs

I have no money, no resources, no hopes. I am the happiest man alive.

—Henry Miller

SLEEPING DOGS

A Novel

Kevin Hazzard

*Mercer
University
Press*

ISBN 0-86554-812-9
MUP/H615

© 2002 Mercer University Press
6316 Peake Road
Macon, Georgia 31210-3960
All rights reserved

First Edition.

This is a work of fiction. While, as in all fiction, the literary
perceptions and insights are based on experience, all names,
characters, places, and incidents are either products of the
author's imagination or are used fictitiously. No reference to
any real person is intended or should be inferred.

The paper used in this publication meets the minimum
requirements of American National Standard for
Information Sciences—Permanence of Paper for Printed
Library Materials,
ANSI Z39.48-1984.

Library of Congress Cataloging-in-Publication Data

Hazzard, Kevin M., 1977-
Sleeping dogs / by Kevin M. Hazzard.—1st ed.
    p. cm.
  ISBN 0-86554-812-9 (alk. paper)
  1. Charleston (S.C.)—Fiction. 2. Male friendship—Fiction.
3. Bus travel—Fiction. 4. Young men—Fiction. I. Title.
  PS3608.A99 S58 2002
  813'.6—dc21
                                              2002008459

For Pep. You've done more than I've asked. You've given up more than I could've expected and you've followed me farther than I ever would've imagined. Thank you.

Reed, thanks for reading and rereading this book and for thinking it was good from the beginning. It probably would've been in the trash without your help.

Milam, thank you for your encouragement and help. Anyone with success has a lucky break and mine was meeting you.

Mom, thank you for never questioning why I wanted to go south and for not being surprised when I took the bus back.

Thanks to my friends whose words make up this book.

Thanks to Kevin Manus for believing in my idea and for bringing it to life.

Book I

When I got to Philly I called Sal. He met me at the terminal in a Hawaiian shirt and a floppy white hat that hung down over his eyes. We carried my bag to his car and shut the doors and were driving past the street vendors and the panhandlers before he asked me.

"So what are you doing down here?"

I watched the city pass through the window and tapped on the armrest. I told him about my job, the one I worked so hard to get but never liked. I told him about how much my hometown in Maine had changed since I left for college and how I no longer loved to watch the waves crash over the rocks and into the streets in York Beach.

He just drove and I talked about my parents being there, but not being there and about how I did not want them there, so close to me, in either sense. I liked college but it was over. The moment was gone. Just like my childhood had been a moment, but it ended when I left Maine and after I returned it was gone.

We talked about my roommates, friends from high school that knew nothing about who I was now, but only what I was when we ran along the slippery rocks and trapped lobsters and floated in the green foam of the night ocean years before. I told him how I woke up smarting one morning after realizing that going home wasn't what I thought it would be and that the moment was gone and then I was packing my clothes and everything else that was mine into boxes and then I threw it all away. I told him about how I stole clothes and money from my roommate and bought a bus ticket.

Spending seven hours on a bus with smelling and sweating people who haven't bathed or slept in hours makes you angry and takes away your hunger, but it makes you want to talk and tell the stories. I told him about the kids who smoked green the whole time and rummaged through other people's bags in a station just outside of Rockport. The short one had heavy black sneakers and no socks and his feet stunk and I was awake and not hungry the whole time and I never said a word, but now I was tired and hungry and I kept talking until Sal cut me off.

"You hungry?" He kept his eyes on the road and never looked at me.

"Yes."

We were in Pittston before the sun dipped down below the mountains in the east and I looked out the window at the trees and the towns in the valleys as we curled around the roads. We stopped in an old taproom that looked like a house with light blue siding on the walls. The screen door was flimsy and creaked when we walked in under the awning and the old sign with chipped paint. The floor was slippery from too much grease and squeaked under our feet. We sat on old stools that were too sticky to spin and a bartender walked out through an open doorway leading to the back room. He grabbed a towel off his shoulder, ran it across the bar and lit Sal's cigarette.

"Eating?"

"Yeah. Can we get some beers—Yeungling Lager—and two burgers?" Then to me, "Will, you gotta try their burgers."

I went to the bathroom and washed my hands, splashed water on my face and let it drip down into my mouth and onto my neck before dipping my face down again and splashing it one more time. I spun the metal crank on the paper towel dispenser, tugged off some paper, and dried my face and hands.

Sal was drinking his beer and talking to the bartender when I came back. We ate without a word and after he finished Sal looked at me seriously. He smiled, hesitated, and then asked the bartender for another drink. Sal watched him pour it slowly into the glass and, after it was in front of him, he picked it up and took a big swallow. Then he looked at me less seriously and said that he was leaving too.

"I'm going to Cali. In a week. Gonna go to Napa and live in the mountains for a while. Come with me."

"What the hell are you going there for?"

"Restaurants, wine." Sal was a computer genius and started working in Cobol and DOS when the rest of us were riding our bicycles and watching afternoon specials. He read too much and he never heard what teachers said and probably learned more than we did with all of our listening. But he never loved it.

"They have newspapers there, you know," he said. "You can work as a reporter for a while—maybe in some cool coastal town. Live in a small place on the beach, surf, eat fruit, and read your books. It would be fun."

But California was too far away. I spent most of my life in Maine, went to college in New York. I never loved the food, not like he did, and Napa might not give me anything that I already didn't have.

"I don't know. Let me think about it, maybe," I said.

"Sure." He knew I wouldn't go.

We spent the next day floating in his pool and drinking beer. He had a greyhound named Romeo who sat under the bushes and ate flowers and drank pool water all day. Romeo moved for no one and Sal laughed about how much trouble he was going to have getting him in the car and driving him all the way to California. It was a long drive and Romeo would throw up going around the block.

I splashed water at the dog and smiled at the thought of him cooped up in the backseat of the car. He turned his long, skinny neck to me and then went back to the flowers and kept eating.

The afternoon sun moved slowly from the east to settle in the west and we watched it go by on our backs, with the pool water drying on our stomachs, floating and drunk. We told stories about college and parties and about people we no longer knew. The afternoon passed warm and happy, consciously unaware of anything. It was a memory before it ever really started.

The wind picked up in the late afternoon and goose bumps ran across my arms and back as I got out of the pool. I grabbed two beers from the cooler and opened them with a towel over my hands to keep the sharp edges of the metal caps from cutting into my pruned skin. I handed one to Sal.

"Tomorrow," he was looking at Romeo who was still eating flowers. "Tomorrow let's go to the Poconos. We'll go down to the river. I'll call Chas and Gerry and we can just hang out."

"OK."

Chas and Gerry went to high school in Pittston with Sal and never went to college, but came up every weekend to meet college girls. It would be good to see them, but for now we were tired. We took naps after the pool and when I woke up my mouth was dry, my head was heavy, and I was exhausted. The evening passed in a blur.

We got Chas and Gerry out of bed at seven the next morning and got on the road into the mountains. I was glad to be out of Pittston. The mountains were green and flashed past the car in a blur. Gerry and Chas talked the whole time, Sal drove, and I just looked out the window and laughed at their stories.

"So the funny thing about all of this," Chas had a hard Philly accent, "is that this woman is bitching about whatever I'm doing, which really was what I was supposed to be doing, and the whole time Gerry's in the backyard clipping the bushes too short and throwing sticks at her dog."

"There's a lesson there, Will. Even if you couldn't get it from this kid's story." Gerry was from the hills, but he talked like Chas from spending so much time with him. "The lesson is that you don't screw around with people who are doing work for ya. Simple."

"So how long have you two been in business?"

"You mean landscaping?"

"Yeah."

"Three months, I think."

"Yeah, we started right when the winter ended. It ain't bad. Gonna be harder in the summer when we're doing yards and it's hot as hell and we're sweating, but it ain't bad. I don't know what we're gonna do in the winter, though."

"Well, the thing is that we can do what we want. This is our business. If we wanna shovel or plow or just get the hell outta here and do whatever, that's cool."

"Are you guys happy? With what you're doing?"

"Hell yeah, man." The landscaping idea had been Chas's and he was excited about it. "We're doing what we want, when we want. Ain't got nobody to tell me when to come to work. We hired some good guys, got a lot of lawns, you know. Some businesses too."

"That's the key—businesses. They always got cash and they don't have some son that's gonna be old enough to mow in two years."

"Well, the thing is, you have to do more than mow. That's why we're getting into landscaping, real landscaping. Ya know?"

Four years and $80,000 had not been enough to buy my way into something that I liked or even tell me what I liked. Chas and Gerry could not name all the Great Lakes, but they had their own business and they loved it.

§

We got to the river around noon and parked the car in a small gravel lot in the middle of a pine forest. The smell of the trees was sharp and cut into your lungs when you breathed, but it was better than the city and definitely better than the staleness of the bus.

"I think the river's down that way, right?" Gerry only came here twice a summer and he was still lost.

"No, no, no. Numbnuts. That way. Christ, if we listened to you we'd still be in the driveway. Shut up and grab the other side of the cooler."

"Chas, I'll kick your ass right now."

"Will you two shut up? For once? Really." They grumbled and Sal looked to me and said, "Will, can you lock the doors?

The keys are in my pocket." He was holding a second cooler and I fished keys out of his shirt pocket and hit the lock button and stuffed them back in his shirt.

"Oh ho. Looks like someone's been hiding smokes." I grabbed a pack of cigarettes from his shirt pocket and stuck one in my mouth.

"You bastard. You been bummin' mine this whole time? Will, give me one of them."

I threw the pack to Chas and he handed one to Gerry and then stuffed the cigarettes back into Sal's shirt and patted him on the chest.

Sal grumbled, "OK, OK. That's great. Just pick that cooler up and let's go."

We skidded down the steep slope of the trail and even with flipflops I scuffed my feet on tufts of grass and bared roots. I got dirt and cuts on my toes and bug bites on my ankles. The sun was full over our heads now and the trees didn't really break the rays that were coming down. Bugs hissed and sang from the grass on both sides of the trail and blocked out some of the yelling between Gerry and Chas.

The river ran across the bottom of a valley, split the trees for a hundred yards across and wound for miles in both directions. We dropped our stuff on the mud and pulled our shirts off and tumbled into the water. The cold current pulled us along the muddy banks past the rocks on the far side. Floating in the clear water in the middle of the stream, the weeds reached up to tickle our backs.

Past the sticks and mud on the edge, Sal climbed up the bank to a small rock formation and jumped into the river. We all followed and jumped off the rocks for a while until we were tired and the shadows were starting to stretch from the base of the trees toward the river.

I swam back to where our stuff was, against the current, and waded until the water was shallow enough for me to kneel in it. I crossed the sticks and mud to sit in the tall grass where I could smoke cigarettes and watch the water pass. Chas and Gerry and Sal followed me out and we sat in the grass and dried in the sun. Chas told stories about times he came to school and stood with the rolling sun to his back and scratched his windblown hair. He blocked the sun from landing on us, but it hit him and outlined him in golden streaks. He fumbled through words and stories and smoked his cigarette and tried to pretend he knew why we were leaving now and why we had left in the first place. We stayed until two then got in the car and left.

℘

By three, we were bored. Following a stream of cars bouncing down a side road led us to a sign for THE MOUNTAIN GATHERING: THREE DAYS OF MUSIC AND PEACE.

We rented a campsite and set up our tent next to a small stream to bathe in the water. Only problem was the campers used the stream as a bathroom and so we jumped the fence surrounding a pool on the neighboring campgrounds and swam and washed.

The rest of the daylight hours went to drinking and talking. Men, women, and children sat on blankets, throwing Frisbees, cooking, and laughing. Some of them sat on the ground with huge water bongs in front of them. As night fell, someone lit a bonfire and a group of guys with guitars sat down and started playing.

I took a deep breath, exhaled the city, and took off my shoes. We sat with women who were holding children asleep on their laps, men rolling joints, and dogs that ran everywhere. Someone was spinning neon-colored glow sticks in the night and the trails wove around in patterns. I lost myself in the random order of the colors and the shapes they made. The evening passed and the fire burned.

When I was a child my parents took us to the ocean and we made fires on the beaches. I'd throw logs in to watch the sparks fly from them as they popped. The waves tumbled on the beach and when the tide was out they were far away, constant, dull, rhythmic. When the tide was in the waves crashed fast and close together.

In the morning, I'd wake to the smell of burnt wood in my dirty hair and in my clothes. My hands smelled like it and when I showered I could taste the wood in my mouth as the water dripped from my hair. That smell still reminds me of the ocean and the tumbling waves rumbling far off at a low tide. Those memories rolled over me as I watched the glow sticks twirl and listened to the twang of the guitar and the sound of the wood crackling and the dogs barking.

Stiff joints from the night air and the hard ground greeted me in the morning. I unzipped the tent and stood outside on the dew-covered grass to watch the smoldering fires and the few people that were already awake and cooking breakfast. Another loud pull of the zipper and Sal stood outside, handing me a cigarette.

"I think it's over now."

"Yeah," I said without looking at him. "But at least we won't have to listen to those two bitch."

We stood in the quiet of the morning for a few minutes before Chas and Gerry came out and started arguing again. We packed our stuff back into the cars and drove out of the mountains and back into town.

After Chas and Gerry left us to go mow lawns and whatever else made them happy, it was just Sal and me again, wilting on his couch. The tap-tapping of rain on the windows was lulling us to sleep when the door popped open and a tall girl with tanned skin walked in. She dropped down on the couch and pulled her bare feet under her, smiled at Sal and introduced herself to me. You could see in their faces that I was a third wheel.

"I'm gonna buy a Greyhound ticket south. Time for me to go."

Sal made a half-hearted attempt at convincing me to stay. I refused, so he drove me to the bus station.

"Where you gonna go?"

"Don't know. A beach. Anywhere."

"Gonna get a job?"

"No. I'm gonna run away. What kind of runaway gets a job?"

"A broke one."

Sal said he knew guys who went to South Carolina. Charleston. They got jobs at restaurants or on the water. It was far, it was close, it was new enough to be different. We half-hugged in the doorway of the station and I tossed my bag over my shoulder and watched his jeep as he drove off.

The call came for the bus south—first stop DC. I grabbed my bag and made my way to the front of the line. Inside, the bus reeked of fake leather, dirty laundry, and sweaty people.

I found a seat halfway to the back of the bus and sat down next to the window, sighed, and leaned my head against the back of the seat. With a plop, a large woman dropped down next to me. The air in her seat burst out into mine and I rose a little and then sunk back down. She was out of breath and her big leg was sticky with sweat and thumped against mine. I pushed closer to the window. She pushed her bag on the floor under my feet.

"You gonna turn on the AC?" she yelled to the driver.

"I gotta wait to shut the door first. Hot out there, I ain't wastin' all my gas."

"It's friggin' hot back here, too."

The driver ignored her and she pushed back in her seat and cursed him under her breath. She swept her long curly hair behind her shoulders with both hands and looked at me.

"Ain't you hot? It's like a damn oven in here."

I smiled a small smile and said, "Yeah, but you'll only make it worse by getting mad."

Satisfied with my drugstore wisdom, she smiled and told me that her name was Tamra. Tamra who had a boyfriend and a job in North Carolina and an ailing mother in Philly. She split her time between them all and the bags under her eyes showed it.

Her boyfriend was Jerome, a construction worker born and raised in Charlotte. They met on a cruise and Tamra quit her job in Philly and moved to Charlotte to be with him. He was a good guy. She loved him, but her mother couldn't take the heat, so Tamra traveled back and forth. Bad luck was typical for Tamra. From fourteen on she raised her younger brothers when her mom's second husband took off. Her mother had diabetes and daily doses of medication, regular hospital visits, and needles were too much reality for every man she met.

"So what are you going south for?" Tamra asked.

I told her about how I quit my job and left home without any idea of where I was going. She laughed when I told her I'd never been to Charleston and was shocked that someone could just pack up and go. But what she really couldn't understand was why I had chosen to take the bus. For her the bus was a cross to bear, a sign of her poor background, and she'd much rather have been on a plane with the rich white people she served at the country club.

"So what do you do? For fun, I mean. Do you, like, take safaris and stuff?"

"Actually, this is the first time I've ever done anything like this. This is my first time away from home. I went skydiving for the first time this summer, though. That was fun."

"Skydiving? You're crazy, boy. There's no way I'd do that. I'm scared of planes anyway. No way I'm gonna jump outta one."

"You're not even curious?"

"Me? What? White people stuff—that's what my boyfriend says. White people are always doing crazy stuff. You won't catch black people doin' all that. Too dangerous."

"How about scuba diving or camping or hiking?"

"White people stuff. I don't wanna get eaten by no sharks. I don't like bugs and I walk too much anyway." She looked at me and put her finger up and shook her head.

I leaned back and laughed.

I asked her, "So what else won't you do?"

If it was dangerous or cold or sweaty, it was white people stuff. She never went camping or stayed in dirty places or stepped down a level. She had risen above dirty or broken down or beaten up. To go back meant to step back and she wanted none of it. Her voice was soft, but her pride was hard and she'd bitten down on a cold morning with not enough blankets or not enough food too many times.

Tamra turned away and pushed herself against the arm of the chair and chewed on her gum. I turned back to the window and stared at the mountains until they were out of sight and then watched the cars. I thought about my family and friends and what stories I'd have if I went home. It was all adventure and it made my stomach flutter, the way a child gets standing in the dim light of his living room counting presents on Christmas morning.

℘

Squealing brakes woke me up as the bus jerked to a stop. Bags, soda cans, shoes, and a Walkman slid up the aisle, some of it making it far enough to hit the front and tumble down the stairs to the door. I sat up and looked around. The early evening sun was low enough to splash through the windows and the bus was golden and blinding. Everyone was confused and asking questions. I tried to relax but the bus was getting hot again and Tamra started to fidget and pushed her sweaty thigh against mine.

"Looks like we got some traffic coming into DC," the driver yelled over the intercom.

"No shit," yelled the man who had been slapping his crying son in the terminal back in Philly.

"We're only about thirty miles from the beltway, but it looks like it's gonna take some time to get there."

"You've gotta be kidding me." Where were we? Not even to DC?

"That's nothing," Tamra said. "You know what that means on the Greyhound? It means we're gonna miss the connection in DC. And that means we're gonna have to catch another bus when we get there. But everything will be delayed. I bet it's another day to North Carolina."

And so we sat. After an hour the driver told us to get out and stretch our legs. I leaned against the back of the guardrail with Tamra and we smoked cigarettes and traded stories about home. We had nothing in common and yesterday we never would've said a word to one another. But there, on the side of the highway, thirty miles outside of DC, we were friends. I leaned back and smiled as the sun shined on my face. *I could be at work right now staring at my computer*, I thought as I flicked the cigarette into the street.

Next to us, the driver sat on the guardrail listening to his portable radio.

"Aw, man. Damn," he said looking at the radio. "We're gonna be here all night." Then he looked up at us. "Some guy got shot in the head in his own damn car. Some kind of drug deal or something. Hell, by the time they clean that mess up, it'll be morning."

My heart sank. I couldn't believe it. We hadn't even really started.

"Are you serious?" I asked him. "I mean, shot in his car?"

He flashed a gold-toothed grin and slapped his knee. "Welcome to DC, son."

We passed time sitting on the grass in the median with the empty cans and broken bits of plastic from traffic accidents that were swept off the road. We told dirty jokes and tried to guess where the other passengers were going. The bus moved forward a little bit in the beginning, but that stopped when the police arrived and quartered off the highway as a crime scene. It took more than an hour to get a new route.

Sitting there I could taste the exhaust and dust and listen to bus riders arguing with car owners. And there I sat. Waiting. Listening to the sounds of anarchy. The fighting, looting, and loathing. Well, not so much looting. Tamra sat quietly in the grass and watched the light blue run across the sky to the west. I threw rocks at the bottles and smoked cigarettes and was happy I was in the dirty grass instead of my clean office.

☙

We made a handful of stops before DC and a bunch more after and, to be honest, I can't remember which were first. Richmond, Fredericksburg—they were mostly names I knew from four years as a history major. At one stop, a French traveler got on the bus, with a backpack strapped across his skinny shoulders. He sat next to me. Quietly, politely. Nothing like Tamra, who moved out of my life to steal a row for herself.

We spoke sporadically in French. He raved about Paris. I nodded and smiled because I was never that good at French and couldn't really understand. The bus stopped again. People shuffled out through the back doors and in from the front door. Two Africans got on and sat across the aisle from us.

They were tall and thin and the way I expected them to look, except that they were dressed in collared shirts and khaki pants. They spoke their native language and all at once there were conversations in three different languages.

"Cannes, c'etait belle, non?"

"Oui." It was half-hearted and didn't speak of my love for the city I'd met on a high school trip, but I was interested now in a different conversation.

"So you boys are from Africa, huh?"

"Yes." Their answers were quick and polite and spoken in the colonial English I'd only heard in movies.

"So you're tourin' DC, hmm." The man was in his fifties with gray in his curly black hair and beard. He had paint on his shirt and his pants and even on his shoes. He asked what part they were from and started back up almost before they finished.

"I'm from here, really. Family came from a cotton field in Georgia and then went to work in Virginia. My great-great-grandfather killed a white he caught taking wood. Plantation owner helped him since he had saved his wood and sold him up here to DC and saw to it his family made it up before the war started."

He was proud and leaned back and pulled a snuff can from his shirt pocket and sniffed it off of his thumb.

He turned to the second man. "I'm the family storyteller." Then, to both, "Been a tradition among blacks here for generations. The history has never been written."

To keep his audience he breathed deep and talked loudly, putting his hand on the near man's leg.

"See, the second son on my mother's side has always been appointed. We go to a reunion every year and the storyteller tells the history through tales, songs, and dancing. A lot of African-American culture comes from these stories."

I turned my attention back to thoughts of the pebble-strewn beaches of the Mediterranean and cool, dark evenings in tiny French towns like Annecy and when I looked back the talk had turned to politics.

"If you come here and wanna see the real America, not the America Bill Clinton wants you to see with the monuments and the museums, you've got to go to the gittoo."

The foreigners nodded their shaved heads in catatonic intervals and listened.

"In the gittoo, people care about you. If you stand on the corner even once and then don't show up for a week, people'll come an' find you. They'll be concerned. If a man doesn't know you, he'll let you drink from his bottle and he'll call you brother and look out for ya."

"Pense-tu que Paris est la plus belle ville?" asked the Frenchman.

"Oui," I said, only half-listening.

"You can't come here to the capital to see the real America," said the American.

"Et si tu parles francais les gens sont gentile?"

"Oui," I said again.

"No, sir. You've got to leave there to meet the real people in hidden America. You've got to go to the gittoo."

※

It can't be said for sure if what Conway found in Shangri-La was just that or if it had been misunderstood or if the whole thing was imagined, but in the very early hours when dew and the darkness are new, the atmosphere in a bus station can't be understood by anyone who hasn't been there. I drew this comparison somewhere in the mountains of North Carolina, early on the morning of the second day of my bus trip.

I woke up sweating and hungry on a bench at the far side of the station and put my boots on. The sun hadn't even risen and the orange lights of the terminal lighted it the way a fire lights the blackest hours of darkness. In the bathroom a man stooped under the hair dryer, fully naked and I didn't care. He got on the bus just before Jersey and so I knew him.

"Friggin' buses. Ours is late, you know."

"Really?" I hadn't known.

"Hell yeah. That means another group will be here then and we'll have to fight 'em to board."

The whole damn thing was endless, with distractions and diversions. There was nothing you could do but not care.

"Oh, hell, I'm sorry," he said, jumping to the side. "You wanna wash too? Here, I'll move my stuff."

He did and I washed. In the bathroom of a bus station with perfect strangers moving in and out I washed and then stooped under the hair dryer. When I finished, I dressed and walked up the tile-covered stairs to the lobby and ate.

The guy from Jersey was right and twenty minutes before our bus arrived, another pulled in and with them came the sun and I took one last look at Shangri-La and crushed out my cigarette.

Just before the buses revved up their diesel engines and coughed black into the morning, we were called inside. It shouldn't have surprised anyone when they told us that our bus was cancelled or delayed. It didn't matter. It wasn't here. Only we were here. With no way out. Enough was enough of the games. It was time to fight.

A woman stepped out of the roped enclosure for passenger connections to Charleston and started to scream. Her shoulders trembled with rage. "Aw, no! You done left me before! I bought this ticket and it's not my fault you overbooked!"

Her eyes bore a hole through the crowd and into the woman behind the ticket counter who passed the blame onto the man on the other side of the door with a nod of her head.

Banging on the glass she yelled, "I'm gonna kick somebody's ass if I miss my grandson's birthday. Now this just ain't right."

We were all behind her in spirit if not in body and things might've gotten out of control if a second bus hadn't come along to carry the leftovers. But it came and we left North Carolina behind us.

℘

I'd been in Charleston a day when I met Mason. He graduated the year before me and got a job driving one of the horse drawn carriages that the tourists loved because it made them feel like they were really in the Old South. We sat and talked and drank bad coffee on the sidewalk while the sharp stench of horse urine washed over us from inside the stables. I told him that I was trying to be a writer and wanted to experience the South so I hopped a bus and here I was.

The shyness was gone and I told him right off that I needed a place to stay and that I'd make a quiet roommate if he had somewhere, even the floor, that I could sleep. I said I'd give him what little cash I had. He brushed a dirty hand in the air and said I could stay with him. Free. Then he jerked his head around.

"Did you say you were a writer? Of course you did. I know someone. He's a writer, too—a Yankee that went to college with me. He's from New York. Everyone knows him. He's a little loose—I mean he's not easy to handle. I think he's, yeah, yeah, he's in town. He went to Florida with some girl for a few days, but he's back now. I can introduce you tonight."

Then he said that he had to take the horse out for the day. So I went with him. Six days a week he drove that carriage through the same congested streets, giving tours and explaining the historical significance of the same buildings each time he passed. He had to wear tan pants, a white shirt, and a red scarf and speak with a thick accent for the tourists. It was fake, but the passengers loved it. I fell for it too, but only for one round. God only knows how he did that six or seven times a day. I jumped off the back and spent the day wandering Charleston.

At six o'clock I made my way back to the carriage house and found Mason washing his horse. He smiled.

"Oh, hey bo," he said.

"How was your day?" I asked.

"Oh, uh." He looked back at the horse. "Well, you know. You were there. Work is work, you know? Going fishing this weekend, though. My folks got a thirty-five-foot sport fish."

"A what?"

"Sport fish. A boat. It's nice. You need to come out sometime."

He finished with the horse and walked it back into the stable. I scraped my fingers along a palm tree and stared at the buildings and the gold in the sky. I thought about Tamra and North Carolina and wondered if she'd ever think of me and if she'd ever try skydiving.

Mason and I walked down the uneven sidewalk and into the market where the shopkeepers were putting away their tables and crafts for tomorrow. The city was different at night, when the bars were crowded and the horses asleep. We went to a restaurant with a patio full of chairs and tables. There was a bar in one corner and the huge vats of the micro-brew in the other. At the gate a woman collecting the five-dollar cover charge and a police officer met us. We paid our money, flashed our IDs, and went in. We walked to the bar in the corner opposite the vats and ordered two pints.

"There he is." Mason yelled to his friend and tossed his empty cup in a bush as he walked to the fence. "Harry! You're late."

"Huh? Yeah, well, we gonna go get a drink?" Harry was jumpy and nervous, his hands fidgeted and his head swiveled on his thin neck.

"Yeah, come on in."

"Not here. Let's go to Dengate's."

We were out in the street and moving toward the water before Harry asked me who I was.

"Will's a writer. I met him this morning. He's gonna stay with me while he's here," Mason said as he pushed between us.

"How long you here for?"

"I don't know," I said. "I came here on the bus."

"The Dog!" Harry screamed. "I love the Dog, it's the only way to travel. It's dirty, slow. Those are the lowest people on earth, you know—my kind of people. I love the Dog. It's the only way I travel."

Harry wore plaid shorts and striped shirts and white socks with red stripes pulled up to his knees. He had old, blue sneakers and no rhythm. He chain-smoked any cigarettes he could find and kept a dozen in a silver cigarette case that he carried in his pocket. His voice was deep and loud and articulate and he held none of his opinions to himself.

On Sunday mornings he went to a local diner to hold court for a captivated audience of self-proclaimed intellectuals who spent their time spitting back Harry's opinions to anyone who might think them smart for it. Sometimes, late at night, he conducted his Sunday morning ritual at other diners, with a darker audience. This is what he lived for.

He looked at me one morning during one of his tirades and leaned over the table and told me that he was an enigma.

"Someone's likely to shoot me at any time." He flipped back up in his chair because he thought the waitress was leaning in to listen. He spilled his coffee on the floor and when she bent down to clean it up he leaned towards me and said that he sometimes suspected her in the plot and then laughed and turned to her and began apologizing profusely.

He spent his days walking around the town—he never learned to drive—and talking. In a town seething with Southern pride, a homely, rude Yankee with a bad wardrobe strutted around like a peacock and was permitted liberties I would have been shot for. He was too good to miss so they tolerated him.

"Hey, you got a smoke, boss?" Harry asked me.

I reached in my pocket and pulled out my cigarettes, handed one to him, and took one for myself. I exhaled and was looking around at the cobblestone streets and the ancient buildings that made the cars seem out of place when I heard a scream. Looking over, I saw Harry shaking his hand and cursing the matches. He burned his finger, a symptom of his accident-prone life, a curse that met him at birth and stuck him with all his family's worst genes. He laughed about his burnt finger and pulled a lighter from his pocket and carelessly lit his cigarette.

Sitting on Harry's couch, I could hear his porch swing as it creaked in the breeze. Harry's was the upstairs apartment. Below was a young couple who had become friends of his like everyone else. Both apartments had a porch that ran the entire length of the house—the left side if you were standing in the street looking in.

I had gotten up early that morning and left Mason's place after he went to work and wandered over to Harry's. Since his was the upstairs apartment, Harry's place was split into three levels. One big main room and two tiny levels with ceilings so low you had to crouch. Above the main room were three small bedrooms and below was a closet-sized bathroom. The main room had a kitchen that opened into a den. The apartment was old and someone sitting quietly on the porch could hear anyone inside walking around the main room, climbing the stairs to the bedrooms, or walking down the short flight of stairs to the bathroom. The den was lined with bookshelves, stuffed and overflowing, and on the floor were pages, covered front and back with handwritten notes.

"What is all this?" I asked, picking up a paper and sitting back on the couch.

Harry was in the kitchen mixing a Bloody Mary and ignored the question.

"Really? That's great," I said when he sat down.

He mumbled something as he sipped his drink and flipped through volumes of the collective works on James K. Polk.

"What?" I asked.

"What?"

"I said, 'What is this?'"

"Stuff. Read it and see."

I read it and it was poetry and prose and songs and it was good. We argued over whether or not he should publish his work. He insisted the world would never be ready for a Chicago

University graduate who read and reread the Bible, but only in Russian. I told him he was kidnapping some of the best work I'd ever seen as he mixed me a Bloody and started holding court.

By noon the Bloodys had turned to vodka gimlets without warning and the Stolis and Rose's lime juice started to fall hard on an empty stomach. Friends came to hear and talk, but I was too drunk to notice who they were.

"The notion—the absolute and undeniable brazenness of it is what kills me—that a high school dropout would stand up and take the fate of the Western world into his own hand, the Black Hand as they called it, is unbelievable." Harry was really getting worked up. "I mean, the arch duke and his driver never expected Mr. Princip to do what he did."

"I think it was great and he should do it again," someone answered.

We all laughed, except Harry, who took another drink.

The room was smoky and dry and too full so I walked outside to get some air. I could only take so much of eighty-year-old international politics.

Charleston is a peninsula, surrounded by islands, bordered on either side by two brackish rivers. The ocean is a long drive from the peninsular downtown and the trip made me nervous considering the two empty bottles of Stoli sitting on Harry's counter.

Harry was in the back of a beat-up Isuzu pick-up. I was in the backseat of Jack's silver Olds. Jack was another Northern transplant and a better drunk driver than a sober one and as we cruised over the wild marsh grass under the cement connector, he danced in his seat, pumped his fist to the music, and almost never checked the road.

"From Maine?" asked someone sitting in the front.

"Yeah. You?"

"Nowhere, really."

Jack clarified, "He's a Navy brat. Lot of those in the South."

Jack laughed and pointed to the truck. The guys riding in the bed were pretending to surf while Harry pretended not to notice.

The beaches in South Carolina are not the dreamy blue ones honeymooners flock to, but they are natural and bordered by dunes and wild grass and I liked them. We parked in the line of cars on the edge of the beach, grabbed our coolers, and walked across the dunes and onto the hot sand.

Everything on the beach was quiet and the haze made the air gray and all the colors soft like an old photograph. Jack dropped our cooler next to six others. They all had rebel flags painted on the sides.

"I never understood this crap," he said, pointing to the flags. "Half of these kids don't have family that were here then and even if you do, why would you be so proud of an ass-kicking?"

"Maybe because they said they weren't gonna listen and they didn't. Maybe just because it looks so damn cool," I said.

Jack laughed and propped a radio against the rocks and sent the sandpipers scattering across the sand on their short legs. As I was loving the newness of the Southern accent, my hard R's and blended words were becoming all the rage.

"Say, 'Park the car.'"

The guys laughed and the girls blushed and suddenly I was the number one fan of my uniqueness. The afternoon passed dreamily and silent beneath the alcohol. Then the wind skipped across the sand with a cool hand and there was the first sign of evening and the afternoon was gone. With browned shoulders and a red face, I jumped into the front seat of Jack's Olds.

A long ride from the beach in a hot and humid car is one of the closest things to hell on earth. Our faces greasy with sweat, our backs salt-sticky and raw from the sun, we stuck to the plush upholstery of the car. But back in town I got the coveted invite to Harry's apartment—known simply as Harry's—and even as nice as Mason was, I never left.

Days were a blur and so were nights, but you never forget the feeling of showering with a warm buzz after spending a drunken afternoon with friends on the beach and flirting with girls. Dressed, freshly tanned, and starting round three, the house was alive with laughter as we shared the bathroom and tips on which girl was giving who the eye. Harry was impervious to the seductions of a battle he wasn't assured to win and listened with secretly open ears. I always tried too hard and came home alone.

By ten we were on the porch—shorts, sandals, and shirts looking better than usual under blue lights and tanned faces framed by windblown hair. The girls they knew were tested and true and arrived at 10:30 and sometimes brought girls who nobody knew and who didn't always stand up well. A cocktail hour started with tequila shots in my honor and degraded to body shots on the tight belly of a girl Harry said he wouldn't touch with a stick.

We went out to bars and danced and drank and then went to the beach and talked on the sand and swam. The water was warm and wrapped the blackness up to my chin so I couldn't even see as far as my feet.

"But you know there are fish down there," Jack yelled when we were too far out to even swim down to the bottom. Just to think of them gave us the chills so we pulled our feet up.

On the sand the cold breeze dried the salt to my skin while we listened to the rumble of each wave and the sizzle of the water turning to foam on the sand then rolling back under the next wave. Shining on the water, the moon sat like half a face, leaving the sky to the stars and the rest to the black horizon just past where the water broke and crested white.

Harry's friend Alex was there with a white shell necklace and curly hair that tossed in the wind. Alex lived in Charleston and never worked. He just lived. His parents picked up the tab for a car and an apartment and for him there was only the beach and the sun and the girls. He smiled the easy smile of a warm and lengthy childhood and loved Charleston and always said "thank you" for nothing.

"How long have you been here, Alex?" I asked as I leaned back and dug my hands into the cool sand.

"Don't know."

He finished a Corona, shook the bottle, and watched the squeezed lime bounce back and forth on the bottom.

"Jen, can you hand me another beer?" He smiled at her and she kissed his forehead and walked over to where her roommate and Jack were sitting. He smiled at me and nodded his head toward Jen. "Nice. Um, I don't really know, man. To be honest. It's just a place and I think I'll be here for a while more. Just don't know how long."

"You're lucky."

"I know." He laughed and shook his head. "Lord knows my mama is too good to me. It's good, though—I'm glad."

℘

The only thing worse than living with an early riser is living with a late riser. Harry was a late riser. The big clock in the main room rang nine as I stepped out of the shower, still trying to shake off a growing hangover. I would've drunk my way through it with a Bloody Mary but I kicked over the last bottle of Stoli while stumbling through the kitchen. The door opened before I finished cleaning up the mess.

"Will, is that you?" Alex was standing in the doorway with coffee in his hands.

"Yeah. You always up this early?"

"Nah. I'm up today, though. You got cigarettes?"

"Yeah."

"Good. Grab 'em and come on."

"Where to?"

"The magical mystery tour. Where do you think?"

We drove down Calhoun Street to Marion Square, a small park at the base of the historic district, and parked on King. The city is a maze of roads reaching from the crowded and dirty streets of north Charleston to the sandy roads along the beach.

The city smacks of antebellum South like so many others, but Charleston is the only one that looks real enough to pull it off. Between the buildings and the streets, nothing modern looks right there. Confederate flags flap against the outer walls of the shops that sell them alongside pictures of Robert E. Lee and Scarlett O'Hara. Countless museums are dedicated solely to "The War of Northern Aggression" and schools spend months on end studying it.

The center of Charleston is the market where slaves were sold when they outnumbered freemen. Today, hoards of women, large and watchful, sit in the market, weaving endless piles of straw into baskets. The stale smell of horses fills the air. Carriage drivers stand on the curb in their white shirts and their gray pants with their Confederate hats on their heads and run hoses along the gutters to wash the piles away.

Restaurants line the roads and mix with the open markets and the animals and the salt blowing in from the harbor so that the air is alive. It fills your nose and runs down into your mouth until you can taste the food and remember why it was that you came here.

But the heat and humidity are oppressive in the summer. The thick air chokes your lungs and makes your hands wet and the sweat stays on your skin and soaks into your shirt and your pants. Your clothes stick to your skin and there's only the sweat even at night. It was so thick my glasses fogged whenever I walked outside and the few envelopes I brought south sealed themselves.

That's the way it was that morning. Alex and I sat sweating on a bench in the center of the market.

"What time is it?" I asked.

Alex started to answer, but turned his head when he heard the scratching and picking and drumming of a one-man-band.

A man with a drum, symbols, horns, a washboard, spoons, a banjo, an accordion, and harmonica all tied to his arms and legs danced around the corner. He moved around the growing, confused, half-annoyed crowd, each movement causing one or more of the instruments to start. His music was good only for the novelty of seeing creativity at work.

I turned my back on him as he struck up Dixie. For all of the tourism and the circus acts of Charleston there's something poetic about the eccentricities of it that go unnoticed. No one sees the uneven sidewalks and narrow cobblestone streets and the tiny, lamp-lit alleyways rising and falling like the crash of the surf. At night the streets light up like some place in Europe and by day the waterfront and weather-beaten cemeteries slow the pace beyond hypnotic.

I lit a cigarette and handed the match to Alex as we moved away from the noise.

"We have as much insanity here as anywhere. It's just you notice ours more because of all the niceness."

I didn't even know what he meant. I just nodded.

"Go down King Street, for example. Full of punks and freaks every night," he said. "Everyone's doing coke in the bathrooms of restaurants. Go north and there are people shooting each other in the streets. That's coming here, too—the violence. But south of Broad the people are rich and their Charleston is pretty and they don't see it."

"Why stay?"

"Place is too beautiful. Same reason y'all keep coming down here to visit."

"Y'all?"

"Y'all. Yankees." He smiled. It was the first time that I was ever called a Yankee. And that's what I was—sometimes in endearment, others in hatred, but always a Yankee.

"I know there are more places out there. I've traveled. But I'm from a small town in South Carolina. This is just as good as it gets for me." He flicked his cigarette into the street and ran his hand across the stone wall of a Confederate museum.

"But you could travel. Move somewhere else." We crossed King and started heading north again.

"Been here my whole life. Never moved. All of my friends live here. Nowhere else for me to go."

"What do your parents do?"

"We live on a tobacco plantation up by Myrtle Beach. Always done that. Hell, I don't wanna go back. I like it here. But I can't find a good job where I don't have to work all the time."

"Tobacco?"

"Yeah. Some people call it—." He blushed and laughed and shook his head. "They call it 'backer.'"

I tried not to laugh, but it came out of my nose. I tried to hold it in, but I looked at Alex with tears welling in my eyes. He looked at me and we broke out laughing.

"Who picks it?" I asked after I pulled myself together.

"Well, we hire people from town, blacks mainly, and they do it."

"Where do they stay?"

"Well, we have houses for them on the plantation."

"What do they have in them?"

"I mean, they have running water and a roof over their heads. What else does a nigger need?"

My feet went numb but my legs found the sidewalk and kept me moving. Alex laughed nervously and looked down. He scrubbed his curly-haired scalp with one hand and nervously twirled a cigarette with the other.

"I mean, I'm not prejudiced, not mean. I have a lot of black friends." His voice got stronger. "People just say that word here. I grew up with it. My grandma calls the kids who mow her lawn niglets and they don't even notice." He bit his lip nervously and looked across the street for help.

"It's bad, isn't it?"

"I don't know. I'm not from the same place you are."

"Yeah."

We were quiet for a half a block. We passed a glassed storefront and looked in the windows at the tiny replicas of waterfront houses and flags with Palmetto trees and burlap bags with "GRITS" scrolled across the front that tourists bought to decorate their kitchens.

We sat at a table in front of a café and ordered drinks and I watched the shadows dry up and disappear as the morning turned to noon. Alex narrowed his eyes on the people walking around the streets. Most were tourists, but some lived there.

"What are these people gonna do?" he said with his finger pointed at them. "There aren't any jobs here. What are they gonna do? Nothing. They're gonna stay here and go to the beach and eat at Shem Creek and watch the sun rise over the harbor. And that's what I'm gonna do. Because I can. Because I love it here. Because it's small, and maybe I'm as backwards as this city or maybe even worse, but I like it here and I'm gonna stay."

I watched him spin his glass on the table and twirl it so the ice spun and everything spilled over the edges and dripped onto the table. I watched him do what he wanted to do and I thought that I was where I was supposed to be, but I had no idea where I wanted to go. But he did and maybe he was backwards, maybe he was worse. But he knew where he was and where he was going and he was glad about it. He looked at me after he finished his drink.

"Let's go to Harry's and start making margaritas."

"You ever gonna get a job, Alex?"

He thought for a second and then smiled. "Nah."

℘

When we got back to Harry's he was walking around the room and Jack was sitting on the couch. They stopped when we walked in the door and then Harry turned back to Jack and started talking.

"OK, so if I was famous I suppose I would say something insightful. How about—." He stopped to light a cigarette. He threw the matches down on the table and finished his drink.

"So I suppose I would start off with something insightful."

"Start it off with anything you want. Just start it off already," Alex said as he started to make drinks. "Anyone else want a margarita?" There were yeses all around.

"I would say, 'So I went to the beach, but it was dry and instead I decided to climb a mountain, but got too low so I decided to call it quits and here I am gone again.' That's what I would say."

Alex looked up from making the margaritas. "What the hell does that mean?"

"Are you an idiot, Alex?" asked Harry.

"Me? You're the one talking like a moron. You just contradicted yourself on every line."

"You're brilliant. Really. Jack, remind me why it is we hang around with this prick?"

Jack smiled and finished his drink. I don't think any of us knew what Harry was talking about.

Alex lifted a freshly poured glass. "You know what, Harry? How about I take this margarita and shove it right up your—."

"Oh, shut up and bring me my drink."

"Get off your ass and get it yourself."

"OK. That's cool. Just drop some cash on the table for the drinks."

Alex looked at Jack and then at me and rolled his eyes and carried all four drinks across the room and put them on the coffee table.

We spent the morning watching movies. We started with *A Clockwork Orange*, and Harry laughed the whole time when he wasn't talking. When it was over, Harry jumped off the couch, kicking the coffee table and rattling all the drinks. He ran into the back room and grabbed a foreign film called *Man Bites Dog*. Harry loved it and loved even more that he was exposing us to it.

℘

To Jack and Harry, work was play. It was to everyone they knew except for Alex, who was never going to work anyway so he didn't count. We had drinks at Harry's until noon and then went to work. For them, work was the dock and Jay ran it. He was Jack's roommate and moved to Charleston for a summer, but lost track of time. He never decided to leave and never decided not to—he just stayed. His father was a judge and a democrat and Jay publicly became a socialist. He worked on the water as a tour guide, which was funny because when he got here he hated boats and couldn't read a nautical map.

"So, you got a job?" Jay asked.

"No." I spun my head toward him. "No, I don't, but I need one."

"Work here with me. We need someone bad. Can you show up on time?"

"Yeah."

"OK, OK," said Harry. "Close this thing down and let's go out in the water. Nobody wants to talk about work."

Jay locked up the cash register and the life jackets and left the jet skis in the water, but ran a chain across them and snapped the lock at the end shut. Harry was in the boat sprawled across the bow when Jay got in.

"Harry, get your ass off of there and do something."

"You want this bird to sink? I can't even drive a car. What am I going to do? You need me to pull anchor? I can do that."

"There is no anchor, dipshit. Just shut up and sit there."

"Thank you—really. I think I will."

Jay pulled the throttle back and the motor churned and kicked silt into the water as the boat eased away from the dock. He pushed it forward and wiggled it into gear until the propeller spun again and twirled the water in tiny green circles and we rolled out into the waterway.

"You see," said Harry from the bow as he lit another cigarette, "I am at ease communicating with nature as I am doing now." Then to me, "Come here. Look at the water, the marsh grass. People don't see that we're traveling in space. I do, of course, so don't be afraid."

Jay rolled his eyes and Jack sat on the back with Alex and drank beer from a cooler.

"The sky here, Will. It's blue and you can't see any buildings and the marsh is green and the birds are in the trees and the fish are swimming. You think I'm just being dumb."

"I do," said Jay.

"You would. But the point is that things are what they're supposed to be here. Left to its own, nature is balanced."

I listened to Harry. Everything made sense there, where they worked, out in the water. Blue was blue and work was fun. At home it was different and work was work and nothing made sense. It was just different or at least it was for the moment.

"Do you believe in chaos?"

"I don't know, but I think I have enough insanity in my life," I said.

"That's because you're not insane. Alex told me about your tour of Charleston. Was he insane?"

"Who?"

"The kids, the rebels, the bums, any of them. How about Alex?"

"I don't know."

Jack grinned because he liked it when Harry was making no sense and Alex sprawled on the stern like a cat and reached out for the spray. For the rest of the ride, I spoke with Jay while Harry prophesized to Jack. Jay talked less than Harry and wouldn't tell you certain things about himself, like how he got the name Jay. I figured it stood for something. Harry's did and so did Jack's and Alex's and even mine, but I guess we'll never know.

॰

I got up early one Monday morning to make my last walk by myself before I started working. Leaving Harry's, I made the long walk to East Bay Street and caught a bus north. After a few blocks I got off at the Piggly Wiggly and walked into a

McDonald's for breakfast. Coming from a city, I never thought it strange to be one white among many blacks and walked in like I belonged there.

"Morning. How are you?" My voice cracked slightly from inactivity and dryness, but it was clear enough.

"Hmm. What you want?"

I ate breakfast under a veil of suspicion and growing uneasiness. If McDonald's was inhospitable, the neighborhood it sat in was hostile. Walking on sidewalks took on all new complications and either I was walking the wrong way and they were gonna bump me until I turned around or I was invisible.

I moved unnoticed through the streets and looked at the cinder block houses with cracked and broken doors and porches full of old chairs and bicycles. Lawns were lawns by definition and had no grass and spread dirt into the streets when the wind blew. Overgrown and gnarled bushes spread across some of the porches and hid the chipping paint and weathered boards.

The haze got thicker and I walked past buildings with boarded windows and graffiti painted on the sides. There were old markets and convenience stores with caged windows. People sat out front on old wooden chairs or leaned against the walls. Trash had built up along the edges of the buildings and in the gutters. The sun was high over the street and sweat started to bead up and pull my clothes close to my skin. The heat and the wet from the humidity turned the food in my stomach so I hid from the sun under magnolia trees and the tall oaks that lined the streets.

A group of kids followed me for a block, but stopped when a man behind me yelled. I thought he was yelling for them and turned to look back when he continued after they were gone.

"Hey! What you doin' here?" A skinny man in a jacket and winter hat stepped from behind a tree bordering the sidewalk.

I turned and walked away as he shouted again—this second burst too incoherent to make out. A car whizzed by kicking out thin, foul gray smoke and I crossed the street and turned back toward the main road.

"I said, 'Hey,'" the man yelled again.

More scared than proud, I ran. Ran until his voice faded, ran until my lungs burned and my mouth got sticky with spit. Ran until I wasn't so far from safe, until I was on Jack's porch. Then I pounded enough to break the hinges.

"Will, what the hell are you doing here?" Jack came out in underwear, his hair sticking up, eyes squinting.

"Nothing. Can I come in?"

℘

Late that afternoon we sat on Harry's porch and drank Coronas with sliced lime and gin drinks. Jay squeezed the lime around the rim of the glass and the bitterness covered the cold sting of the gin when you first tasted it.

"This gin is good," said Jay with a puckered face from the lime. "I like it better after I've had a couple of them, though."

"That's because it tastes like crap. I only like the Coronas," said Jack.

I stayed away from the Coronas because they were too filling if you were going to drink them all day. The warm from the gin was in my stomach and on my face. I drank just enough to keep a smile on my face and to make me laugh, but not so much that I was slurring or blurry. Harry was in the bathroom showering. We could smell the soap out on the porch and hear the soft hiss of the palms as the cool evening breeze pushed inland.

We were on the silky blue cusp of evening when it's not day and it's not night and the sun is soft and cool. The air was quiet without all of the cars and the people out. We talked quietly and washed the dirt of the day off of our hands and faces and enjoyed the cleanness and the calm of the changing hour. I took a shower after Harry and put on a clean shirt and shorts. The fabric felt cool and crisp against my skin and I made another drink. Harry and Alex were standing on the porch talking to someone that I'd never met before.

"We're going to Bull Street. You coming?" the new guy asked in the deep, slow accent of the upstate. Then he walked across the porch and held out his hand. "Cal Jenkins. You comin'?" Before I could answer, Cal Jenkins, who shook with a firm hand and always used both names, slapped me on the back and pulled his keys from his pocket. "Come on, you can ride with me."

Cal was trying to get his Ph.D. in English. He loved Charleston and the monthly payments from an inheritance his grandmother left kept him there. He was from Honea Path, in the far corner of the state, but South Carolina's small and informal and no matter where you live you know people from every other part. He moved to Charleston, but went to Edisto Island to spend weekends at his parents' beach house or to another house they had near Myrtle Beach.

Cal's family *was* South Carolina. His father was an investor and always went to Columbia for football games and to tailgate when Cal was in college. Mr. Jenkins had a soft, round face and wore canvas hats with his curly hair flowing out of the sides and back. He wore sunglasses or hung them around his neck with a nylon string. All of his shorts were fishing shorts and he wore them with sandals and white tee-shirts with cigarettes in the front pocket and pictures of marlin or a boat he had fished from on the back. Cal's mother was thin and Southern and called us all "baby" and never had to work. Cal decided he'd be my guide.

The street was wet with the humid breeze and my sandals skidded on the slick sidewalk in front of Harry's. Cal's truck was parked on the next block and Harry was going to ride with us so we waited and listened to him clop down the wooden steps leading to the walkway.

"There'll be a ton of girls here tonight," Cal said as he put in a dip and passed the can around. Harry smacked the can with his pointer finger and pinched three fingers full of dip and wedged them into his cheek. He handed the can back to Cal, wiped the bits of tobacco off on his pants and spit into the street.

"Mostly girls we know from deb balls," Cal said after he mashed the dip back into the side of his mouth with his tongue.

"Don't even get me started on that crap," Harry warned.

"What are you guys talking about?"

"You never heard of debutante balls?" asked Cal.

"No."

"Hell, even Harry knows that. And he's about as Yankee as you can get."

I shrugged and Harry walked ahead so he would not have to listen to us.

"See, debutantes are girls whose parents have money and so they throw these big parties." He glanced at Harry, who wasn't listening, and continued.

"The girls all wear white dresses and the guys get all dressed up and it's a huge thing."

"So what do you do?"

"Well, we escort the girls and it's like a reception with food and everybody dancing and all."

"Do you drink?"

"Oh, yeah."

"Why white dresses?"

"Why not? We condone crimes of passion because they happen in the heat of the moment and maybe we think we would've done the same thing so we pretend we don't notice if we can." Cal smiled. "They're parties, Will. For girls with money. Their mothers had them. Their grandmothers had them. Everyone knows what happens, they just don't talk about it. Perceived innocence is innocence indeed, especially in the South. So you have a coming out party for your daughter and you invite the rest of your faux Southern society. Everyone gets drunk and even if you deserved your white dress at the beginning of the night, you don't when it's over."

Cal said girls had a different place in the South and they only glistened and never sweated. He said the societal roles didn't affect education, but when I was in the South I met more than one educated and outspoken girl from the North who caught people by surprise.

Bull Street, nestled in a posh section of Charleston not far from the exquisite south of Broad area, was filled with, and popular for, a heavy sprinkling of beautiful girls spending money from home. Undergrads, medical students, and waitresses filled several blocks of Bull Street. It was prime property.

Ducking the spindly branches and lush beds of magnolia trees, we walked into a backyard alive with delight. White lights strung carelessly in branches of trees lining the yard made it look like how you imagine Rio. Music and laughter filled the air with an invitation to indiscretion. PJ, made from Kool-Aide, sliced fruit, and gallons of grain alcohol, splashed in tubs lining the porch as torches flickered light on dozens of tanned faces.

The cool grass felt good on my feet after walking on the hot porch all afternoon, and greetings ranging from casually polite to slyly provocative floated down from the deck and across the lawn.

We walked up the wooden steps with their peeling paint and the music loud in our ears. There were couples dancing on the porch. It wasn't the awkward, ignorant dancing we always did in night clubs where nobody knows any moves and we just let the music trick us into spinning and turning. It was planned and even. The couples were sweating, but they swept smoothly across the wooden deck. I asked Cal what it was.

"What?"

"The dance. What dance is that?"

"That's the shag."

The shag. It's reminiscent of the carefree days of their parents' youth and is boastfully taught to all Southern boys by their mothers on the kitchen floor. Knowing how to shag was critical to successful courtship. Ignorance was tantamount to treason so I improvised as best I could, but got more giggles than numbers for my efforts. Still, Cal stuck to his word and introduced me to everyone and I continued to amaze with my decidedly un-Southern accent.

My cup clanked the bottom of a gray tub under the porch at about four in the morning and Cal handed me a beer.

"Hell, I think we lost everyone. There's no one left."

I looked around and he was right. Even the girls who lived there had gone inside or had already left with boys they met that night. We recalled our conversation from earlier and laughed, knowing that the same girls who only glistened under the hot Southern sun sweated like stuffed pigs in the blue light of smoky, music-filled rooms. Secretly they sweated harder in even darker ones.

Cal and I walked through Charleston's silent twilight to the cluttered apartment of a girl he knew. We crawled in through her living room window and ate cold turkey and drank Sprite and never saw the girl who lived there. We shared a twin bed, but I got cramped and slept on the floor.

When the sun came up I woke. Cal's friend was dressing for work across the hall with the door open. I pretended I was still asleep. When the heat finally began to breathe life back into the sandy and cracked streets, we walked back to Harry's.

ꙮ

Jay's dock was long and narrow and poked into the Inter-coastal Waterway from the corner of a small marina. It had warped boards that were buckled from rain and sun. The wood was bleached and brittle from exposure and Jack parked his car in the sandy patches of grass just to the side of it. The railing was chipped and splintered and grabbed at your hands and even harder at your shirt. I caught the tip of my sandal on a loose board and stumbled forward and landed hard on the other foot. Jack laughed and pushed me from the side and I brushed against the railing and pulled my shirt on a sharp splinter of wood.

We sat down under the cover of a hut built from extra wood that was covered with palm fronds and sided with parachutes that were spread out and nailed to the wooden uprights and crossbars. Jay had built benches to line the railing that ran along one side and faced the counter and the built-in saltwater tank that we stocked daily with whatever we caught in a cast net. Milk crates sat under the benches and customers put their shirts and shoes inside. Some put their wallets there even though we warned against it and they usually dropped credit cards or pictures into the water.

The sun was rising over the edge of the ocean, leaving a tiny spot between the beach and the countryside that's calm even when the ocean or the countryside wasn't. The morning was there and the sun would come and it would be over the strip and everything would be golden for a few seconds. The sun would keep rolling and it would pass, but somewhere in between lay the perfect place and for a minute in the early morning you could see the gold. And that is where we were, eating sausage biscuits and drinking orange soda and watching the dew on the wood dry as the sun warmed up.

"Grab a life jacket and we'll go out so I can show you the way." Jay stood up and broke the calm of the golden morning and already the sun was getting hotter and the air was heavier and beginning to move.

"Jack, get off your ass and turn on the phones," Jay said and Jack snorted a laugh the way he always did when his best friend turned into his boss.

We put the boat into the water and I idled the engine while Jay pulled the trailer back up the ramp to park. As we worked, Harry frittered the day away talking to Marvin, who emptied the trash and bummed money for smokes. Jay always gave him five dollars and Marvin would smile the gray-toothed grin of a sometime drug addict.

Marvin was a crack addict when he was younger but was clean now. He walked three miles to work every day and drove an old golf cart around the marina, picking up trash as it rotted in the sun. Jay gave him money for cigarettes because the marina paid him only enough to eat and in return Marvin emptied Jay's trash too.

"The Inter-coastal runs from Maine to Miami. It's got a lot of commercial traffic—large sport fishing boats. You understand nautical conduct?"

"Jay, I don't know anything," I said.

"Good. Me neither."

The waterway ranges from twenty to a hundred yards wide and twists itself through a maze of salt marsh dotted with oyster beds, islands, and sandbars. A number of bays are navigable for small boats, but only during certain tides and even in high tide the sandbars make them impossible if you don't know your way.

Jay wove the boat in and out of several inlets and creeks and by the time he slipped back into the waterway, I was lost. Navigating the wrong way around even a tiny island can spin around a novice. In the midst of splashing water and endlessly waving grass many boats were lost and became stranded with the ebbing tide. Rescue parties were endless and the game warden was omniscient. Markers were my only friends until I memorized the identical and infinite creeks and bends.

The sinking sands, rough waters, and sharp oysters made for a dangerous day, but the beauty I found in the cool sunrises and the calm sunsets kept my spirit high and free. I spent the first day under Jay's tutelage and as the sun rolled west I was caked with salt and gasoline-stained. We pulled the boat from the water and washed it and met Harry and Jack on the dock for beers.

CCR's "Fortunate Son" was sailing across the creek and filling the dock with new life when we sat down on the sandy plank floor. Harry was reading and Jack was squinting into the saltwater tank and trying to get the blue crabs and the ghost crabs to eat the shrimp he caught that afternoon. Passing them, I turned on the freshwater shower and scrubbed off the sand and salt under the dull pulse of the island water pressure. I flipped the red plastic handle and the water got weaker and weaker until it was just a spill on the lip of the showerhead. I ran my hands through my hair and slapped the water off my arms and legs, grabbed a beer, and sat down next to Harry. He looked up and threw his book on the wooden bench, stretched his feet out, and crossed his arms across his chest.

"So you gonna be a famous writer and let me hang with your entourage, Harry?" Jack asked without looking up from the tank.

"The funny thing is that I always thought that I was going to be famous."

"Yeah, Harry, you're gonna be a superstar," said Jay.

"Already am. Now shut up. But I really thought that I'd be a famous writer and I'd travel and die young before my work began to slide." He opened another beer and threw the cap at the trashcan, but missed and it skipped into the water.

"Easy man. Don't go throwing all your crap in there," Jay said. Harry ignored him.

Months later Harry told me that he meant what he said on the dock. He told me about people he'd known that he truly loved, people who touched him with their genius when suddenly he knew he wasn't the one who was supposed to be famous, but them. All he wondered was why he should be the one to remember them and not someone else. I didn't know.

But for now, we were on the dock and the sun was splitting the sky into the light blue west and the dark blue east. To the east it was blue and black in some places and the clouds swirled around each other, some thick and some thin. But the sky in the west was light blue and the clouds were round and white. Harry threw his beer in the trash and jumped off the end of the dock into the water. Marvin walked down and pulled the bag from the trashcan and threw it over his shoulder. I gave him a few dollars and he smiled. He walked back to his cart and got in and rode away.

I sat on the bench and watched the gold on the nameless place between the ocean and the land turn to dark blue. Jay jumped into the water with Harry and Jack followed. A great blue heron landed in the mud and bent his long skinny neck down and ate fiddler crabs and picked at oysters. The outlines of the palm fronds faded from sharp and pointy spikes into one rounded bunch and I stood and dove off the end of the dock.

⁌

I woke early one morning when Charleston was not so new and the ocean a familiar home. I ate breakfast and then Jack came and drove us through Charleston under heavy storm clouds that chased the blue from the sky.

"Think it's gonna rain today?"

"Nah. Here maybe, but it almost never rains on the island." Jack was confident and Harry never broke his stare from the passing cars and never made a sound.

I leaned back in my seat. We rumbled across the narrow Cooper River Bridge as the oncoming traffic passed and shook our car with the wind. Out the window I could see through the rusty steel sides of the bridge, down to the wind-tossed water, and beyond the boats to the horizon across the bay. We met Jay at the marina and argued over who would drop the jet skis in the water.

"Hell man, you're the newest guy. You're doing it." Jack threw a life vest at me and walked back toward Jay's truck.

I kicked my sandals off and skidded down the boat ramp, which was wet and slick with seaweed. The wind danced across the open marina and kicked tiny ripples in the water that splashed on my legs and stomach. I shuddered when it hit me and drew back, but the bottom was too slick and my foot slipped out and I dipped down to my armpits. Jack and Jay were laughing in the truck.

"It's too damn early for this," I shouted as I climbed on top of the bouncing ski.

"Wait until you turn the corner and the wind says hello," Jay yelled and pulled the truck around to get the other jet skis.

By the time I brought the skis around, Jack had parked the truck and was greeting customers and Jay was pulling the boat to the end of the dock. Harry was in the marina store pretending to fax articles to his editor. I thought about him when Jay climbed up the ramp and told me to take the morning tour.

"Jay, I've only done it once."

"Relax. Follow the signs and you will find your way. If you get lost, radio me and I'll help you. And stay to the west. That's where the creeks are. There's nothing but rough water and ocean to the east."

I packed a half-dozen sodas into a backpack and clipped the radio to my vest and we rode out into the waterway. The morning was calm and quiet and the birds were sleeping in the trees when we started. The surface of the water was as calm as saltwater gets and I watched the ripples from the jet skis roll out from under our path and across the water to sway the marsh grass. The engines whined and coughed and the birds flew from their nests into the air one at a time, following each other like dominoes.

We rode through the waterway at half speed and I pointed out great blue herons and porpoises and slipped in and out of the creeks like a local. I pulled the group together at marker 92. We were at the mouth of an inlet leading to Bull's Island.

"So other than that creek to the north, please stay away from the breakers at the end of the inlet. Those are caused by sandbars and if you pull too close you're gonna get beached."

"Are there sharks in here?" asked one of the men on the tour. He had a white tank top on under his life vest and a yellow ball cap and sunglasses tethered around his neck with an old shoelace. I smiled and he pushed his hat back and scratched his head, which was peeling from an earlier trip to the beach.

"Probably, but really only sand sharks so you can swim in the inlet."

His eyes narrowed and then widened when he saw that I was serious and he looked at his daughter and son who were sharing a jet ski and had been trying to tip each other over all morning.

"Will you two go easy on that?" he barked at them.

"When we go ashore," I said, turning from the sunburned man, "please let me guide you in and remember that we have Carolina panthers, alligators in the fresh water reserves, and a lot of snakes, so don't wander too far." It was all partially true and it made the tourists feel like they were really lost on a deserted island, though never far from found. White lies aside, the island was perfect and the bent palms and tall reeds made it look more like Tahiti than South Carolina.

I walked them through the island and showed them how to tell the crabs apart and which shells were good to keep. I waded past my waist in the water, knelt and walked backwards toward the shore with my hands raking the sand. It was an easy way to find sand dollars, which are hard to find and it made me look like a pro. The culmination of the tour was when we curved back around the pathways and landed on the north shore to sit under the curving palm trees and watch the waves crash. A warm breeze crept across the sand and rustled the dead fronds and the hiss and the waves were rhythmic.

I sat in the sand and dug my hands and feet in at the water line. The air was thick, but the breeze kept it from covering me like the choking blanket it could become. As the waves patted at my feet, I sat and drank orange soda and spat the salt from my mouth.

The rustle of the fronds grew as they turned inland. When we rode in the bay was smooth and calm, but now it was starting to froth and gnash like hungry teeth. The breeze got colder and brushed against my face. Air temperature on the far islands will drop more than ten degrees when a storm blows in. I watched goose bumps swell up on my arms and saw the clouds soak up the sun and I ran to the water and whistled for everyone to follow.

Like all fickle ocean storms, it looked at first like it would come slow and give us time to beat the rain. But the temperature was still dropping and by the time we hit the waterway, tiny droplets of rain were stinging my face and hands. The bay was dark and quiet, except for the chop of the waves, and I sucked in my breath when lightning shot across the water and lit up the edge of the island.

Waves pounced the front of the jet skis and pushed them from the sides and slowed us to the pace of the storm. I turned my head to make sure that I had the entire tour and I did, but the salt was stinging my eyes and one of the little girls was crying. The sunburned man had lost his hat to a gust of wind so he shielded his tender scalp with his left hand.

We came straight in, but the chop slowed us and it took thirty minutes. I tied my jet ski to a slip and helped Jay haul the tour onto the dock. They rushed up the ramp and shook themselves off under the leaf-covered shack. When the last tourist was in his car and we were alone we laughed the way all locals laugh at tourists who complain because nature's theme park ruined a perfect day to be outside. The rain got worse and I laughed at Jack's forecast while Jay packed everything on the dock into wooden boxes and latched them to keep the wind from blowing it all away.

The pock-marked gravel lot was a maze of muddy holes and as I pulled the hood of Jay's yellow rain jacket tight over my head, my bare feet squished down into the soft mud between the stones. Inside the store Harry was sitting at the far table under a lamp shaded with nautical flags. He was reading and didn't notice me.

"What is this, Eliot?"

"Yeah, we call it poetry. Don't they read in that state of yours?"

"Nope." We sat there for a second before I started again. "Cal was reading Sassoon. Jack had Hemingway and you're reading Eliot. What are you guys, the lost generation?"

Harry looked up for the first time.

"Actually we're hopelessly found. I think we're just trying to get lost. That's why we came here. Half are rich, half are dirt poor, and half have had their heads in their asses for a hundred and fifty years."

"That's too many halves," I said.

Harry looked out the window as lightning lit up the parking lot.

"You're brighter than you look."

A clap of thunder came and shook the thin pane of glass next to our table.

Jay walked inside and sat with us while we talked but Jack stayed on the porch to smoke cigarettes with Marvin. Jay told stories about his dad and about getting lost while taking his parents on a tour last summer. I laughed and knew that Jay would be a true friend and he was. At two o'clock the rain was still falling.

"This ain't stopping. I think we gotta go," said Jack over the squeak of his shoes sliding on the linoleum floor.

"I know. Let me call Cal and we'll see if we can go to his grandmother's for lunch," said Jay. Then to me, "You're gonna love her. She's a great cook."

Cal's grandmother lived downtown so we had to drive back across the connector and through Mount Pleasant. We crossed the river again, on the old bridge, and I wiped the fog from the window and watched the boats steam in and out of the port.

Downtown Charleston is below sea level so when we got off the bridge, traffic had slowed to a crawl as cars strained to push their way through flooded streets. It was strange to see waves rippling through the city and cars sitting marooned against the curbs with water up to their tailpipes. Jay warned me against parking on certain streets that were known to flood when it rained hard at high tide.

It was tough just getting to Cal's grandmother on Beaufain Street because most of its access streets were flooded. The heavy wooden door to her house was set back into the stone walls so that you were in a small chamber between the sidewalk and the house when you went in. The entrance was on the ground floor and the only thing fighting off the flooding rain was a pair of six-inch ledges on either side of the entry chamber. She had a black and rusted door handle and matching knocker. As we waited, a couple walked up the spiraling concrete stairs that led to a second-floor house.

"My grandma lives on the ground floor and the upper two floors are another place," Cal explained as we passed through the doorway and stepped onto the slate floor in her small foyer.

The main room opened to the left of the door with the kitchen adjacent to the living room, which ended at the fireplace and the far stone wall. To the right was her den, with only a single light in the corner. It was off, but I inspected the crowded bookshelves in the flickering light of a dozen candles, some placed in steel-framed globes and others sitting openly on shelves.

"Boys!" Cal's grandmother moved in from the fireplace. "I was certain you would come with the rain."

There were hugs and greetings and lunch requests and she welcomed everyone to anything they would like and turned her bright blue eyes on me.

"Good afternoon. I'm Mrs. Pickens."

"Will. Lightfoot. Nice to meet you."

The woman had lived alone since 1974, but made two full meals a day—breakfast at 8 A.M. and dinner at 3 P.M.

"I've made enough for y'all," she said, placing a soft hand on mine and turning toward the kitchen.

We ate fried pork chops, green bean casserole, homemade pickles, cornbread, and sweet tea. I never got the hang of sweet tea, which wasn't a real kind of sweet or maybe it was just so sweet that it ruined the taste. Cal brought wood inside while we sat and talked. Mrs. Pickens played the role of concerned mother, scrutinizing our habits and schedules and greeting each mention of a new love interest with a tentative, "I hope she's a nice girl."

I stood as the talk got bogged down with, "Yes ma'ams," and listened with a half-open ear while studying her photographs, maps, and art. The globe was spinning under my fingers as she joined me and started to talk about her life.

"My husband was rather a collector," she began, emphasizing awkward words and drawing Rs the way only old Southerners do.

"He was an engineer for the army and somewhat of a pack rat, I'm afraid." She paused for a moment as the sights and sounds of a half-century ago came calling. Then with a sigh, she started. "So, he brought home all sorts of rare books, maps, coins, and later, when we had the money, art."

"Were you alone much?"

"Oh no," she said, her facing shining with the excitement of genuine interest. "I went everywhere with him. I have seen the Duomo, had lunch at a café in the shadow of the Eiffel Tower, and have entertained in Soho.

"I would say I have seen the whole of what Western civilization has made. Well, what's left anyway. We went to the Parthenon in spring and, of course, there was Africa. The moon has a different look in Cairo when it shines on the stone palaces, and the music and smell of food rise from the streets."

Our conversation spilled over into dinner, which really was more like lunch anyway. There was passion and vitality in a woman in whom her relatives found only fragility. She was looked upon with negligent reverence and was handled by a tenderness that spoke as much to the treatment of fine china as it did to love.

In my curiosity for her past, she satisfied curiosities in mine. My inquisition was of words—hers of observance and she wasn't alone. Southerners of all ages held me accountable for the rumors long told of Yankees and used our conversations to test their merit while reinforcing myths about Southern hospitality. Mrs. Pickens was no exception. So there we sat like Hannibal and Starling, reciprocating tales of mutual interest.

When lunch was over, she placed a cobbler on the table and pointed to a clock sitting on the mantle.

"Will, you'll be interested to know that wooden clock was carried home from Virginia by my great-grandfather when he returned from the Civil War. He walked the whole way with that under his arm. It was a present for my grandmother. And the clock next to it was made from a special wood we had shipped home from Kamakura, Japan." She paused and smiled and then turned and slipped away as she quietly served the cobbler.

After dinner we said gracious goodbyes and promised to come back soon. Mrs. Pickens touched my hand like a mother and, in a voice more like a teacher, reminded me that I was welcome anytime I wanted to hear more. I promised to return and put the collar of my jacket up and stepped out into the rain.

℘

The Charleston Harbor surrounds the southernmost tip of the peninsula and is bordered by concrete walls that flatten out into walkways fifteen feet above the water line. Piles of rocks line the walls and slip into the water at high tide, then reappear when the water recedes. The rain was beating and the tide was on the rise and as we drove past the rocks were out of sight.

We drove through the streets with the air wet from humidity, even with the rain, and the sky gray and the stone and stucco buildings cold and brittle. Normally, I loved walking down the narrow streets with the stone buildings running into stucco ones, into brick ones, into wood without a break. But in the rain the feeling was gone.

Jack pulled his car into the driveway and we jumped out and ran inside. I heard the zip of Harry's shoes slipping across the wet stairs behind me before I got inside and the thud of his knees hitting and his shins scraping. He screamed as he fell and Jack grabbed his arm and pulled him up. The door to the downstairs apartment opened and Aaron poked his head out.

"Sweet. You guys are back?" he yelled over Harry's whining. "We brought some food from the restaurant. Should we bring it up?"

"Yeah," yelled Jack. Harry was still cursing the rain and his knees and the painted wooden stairs. "We got beer, just bring up the food."

Aaron and Ann had been married for two years. Aaron was from Long Island and Ann was from New Jersey and they came to capitalize on the South's total lack of great Italian food. Aaron finished film school and asked Ann, whose father ran a restaurant in New York, to marry him. Aaron had wanted to write for *Rolling Stone*, but gave up to get a job and fulfilled his dreams by writing a film review column for a local paper. Ann fulfilled hers in other ways. We ate cold ziti and antipasto salad.

"This food is so good," Jay said with his mouth full of ziti.

"Thanks, Jay." Ann smiled.

Aaron glared.

After dinner, we sat on the couch, the chairs, the floor, and the counter and drank beers and talked. Aaron's eyes smiled as he looked at Ann who was dreaming.

"So tell me about this ghost," Harry said, after an awkward pause. "I've been here about a year and nobody ever told me the whole story."

The rain was coming down hard and the thunder rumbled as the wind kicked chairs around the porch.

"Well, here's what I know," began Aaron as Cal sat beers on the table. "When I first came here, the guy who lived in your apartment was cool, you know. Totally normal. We hung out a little bit, not much but enough to think he was a cool guy.

"So we come home one night and the kid's in the friggin' street with a knife in his hand—and he's screaming—I mean *screaming*." The excitement in Aaron's voice was growing. "So I'm like, he's crazy or going crazy or killed someone or something. So I go out and yell to him and he's almost in tears. And he's talking about noises or something. I mean, I'm not a big ghost person or anything, but he's making me nervous. And if for no other reason than that I'm just scared of him. I mean, he lives above me, remember."

Jay made a joke about Harry not being much better. Ann smiled. Aaron continued.

"Yeah, well when I finally calmed him down he told me he heard footsteps on the porch going up and down the stairs. So, I give him a drink and get him to relax and the night passes. A few days later I go the library and sure enough, some woman was killed right there." He pointed outside to the porch stairs. "Trapped by a fire. Well, I've never seen anything, but that guy was gone. What was his name?"

"James," Ann answered immediately.

"Right. Right, James. Yeah, anyway, that's the story."

"So did you ever see him do anything weird, Ann?" asked Harry.

"Well—."

"Yeah." Aaron jumped in. "The guy came over one night looking for me because he heard something again but I was out. So he stayed with Ann until I got back and then went back home. He was pretty quiet though."

Jack and I went to the kitchen to get beers and he asked me how Aaron never saw what we saw when it was so obvious what Ann was doing.

"Maybe the reality's so hard to face he can't admit it to himself," I said.

My favorite view in Charleston is from the top of the last bridge on the Isle of Palms Connector. It comes after the two-mile stretch of marsh grass and gray cement with metal girders that thump under your tires in rhythmic, two-second intervals. The first time that I saw it I was numb. We had sped across the connector, with the girders keeping time, and climbed the steep slope of the bridge that lifts the connector high enough for the sailboats to get under it with their high masts. Then we were on top of the bridge and the ocean unfolded, gray and quiet. The beach sprung from the cement and the ocean from the beach and the waves were rippling in the distance and the shrimp boats lined up on top of them and it was all there and I was looking and the sun was not high, but low over the water. We looked down on it all from the bridge, for a second, as we passed the peak and then sank back down to sea level.

If you stop and stand on the peak you can see the small beach houses and beyond them the hazy ocean and the shrimp boats. To the right and left reach the banks of the waterway lined with thick clusters of trees. Behind you the miles of marsh grass are dry and forbidding at times, flooded and swaying at others. Beyond the bridge lay our marina and the boats and jet skis and the infinitely inquisitive tourists. Some afternoons the tourists came to ride the banana boat and I became the banana man.

"It's easy, Will." Jay was a master con man and Jack and Harry were jackals who loved to watch him. "All you have to do is pull the thing. It's like a ski trip."

"What the hell am I supposed to do? Where do I take them?"

"Just take 'em to a wide part and spin 'em around," Jack said. "It's cake, really."

"Then you take 'em, Jack."

He just smiled and leaned against the counter.

"Don't worry. It's easy."

I worked the foot pump and inflated the banana while Jay talked to my banana boat riders about how to get back on the banana if they fell off. I watched the group in between pumps and couldn't hear over the swooshing sound of the air filling the rubber pontoons that ran along the side of it, but I could see them smiling and laughing and Jack sarcastically giving me an "OK" sign. I finished pumping as they walked down the ramp buckling their vests and kidding each other about who would make the group fall in first. It was a family of four: the mother and father were in their fifties, their son was about seventeen, and the daughter was about thirteen. I was already feeling guilty.

"Are there alligators in there?" asked the father as he stepped down from the dock and straddled the banana.

"None that bite."

"How about sharks?"

"If we're lucky."

A school of porpoises swam by as I towed the fifteen-foot rubber banana boat into the waterway. I idled the engine so they could watch the porpoises play and swim. They popped their heads out of the water to breathe and watched the great irony of the tourism business: the fact that it preys on families while employing the polar opposite to family—wayward children wanting adventure and to breathe deep of exotic places, anything but to be with their families. We were taken for experts with a full understanding of the ocean, marine life, safety, and first aid. And I was their expert, equipped with a two-way radio, a can of orange soda, spark plugs, and three bandages that Jay always kept in the waterproof Pelican case. Once we cleared the marina, the seventeen-year-old gave an enthusiastic thumbs-up. I hit the gas.

Everyone was silent when I pulled back to the dock. Jay came down when he saw the look on their faces. The father stood and winced, nursing a bruised rib, and helped his wife who had lost her glasses and was moving gingerly on a swollen ankle. Their daughter cursed under her breath and through a fat lip.

The seventeen-year-old who had encouraged me to speed up to thirty—bananas should never be pulled faster than nineteen—had a red stripe across his chest from landing crossways on the tow rope.

When they were gone I told Jay about how they begged to go faster and so I did. I told him that I went over a boat wake and the banana flipped like it always did, but at thirty it was different. We laughed as more tourists walked down the dock for a 12:30 banana ride.

Early in the afternoon I took a tour to Bull's Island and beached the skis far enough on the sand to keep the surf from carrying them away, but not so far that they'd get stuck. The tide was in and the waves were heavy and the sand was thin. I left the tour looking for shells and took off my life vest and hung it on the jet ski.

The water was warm and splashed against my chest as I waded into the inlet and when the sand began to slip out from under my feet I dove in and swam for a few seconds underneath with my eyes closed. The current in the inlet was strong and if you started far enough up, you could let it carry you across the water to the other island and then back again.

I always became conscious of the sharks I shared the water with when I was in the middle. I turned on my back to let the current carry me, but also to keep my feet from dangling into the deeper water. The island facing Bull's had a narrow beach that dropped off quickly because of the tide, but it was more remote and natural. I walked to the front where I couldn't see the tour or the inlet and sat in the sand and watched the shrimp boats go by.

I'll bring them out there, I thought as I stared at the boats half covered by the afternoon haze. They made huge loping waves and the jet skis would glide over them as we watched. Then I thought better of it and jumped back in the water and swam across to tell the tour it was time to go.

I was going to take them straight back, but there was a woman in her forties with long black hair that hung down to the open back of her bathing suit. She had long, tan legs and smiled widely when I told stories about turtles and boats and people who had gotten lost. Her daughter was sixteen and competed with mom for attention, but it was hard and she lost most of the time. The mom asked me if we were going anywhere else and she smiled, shifted the weight of her body onto her back leg and kicked in the water with her front leg.

"Of course not."

We left the inlet and rode serpentine back through the waterway and around the markers. We were nearly in the full moon and the tide was flooding higher than usual, so I brought them through a side stream and then back into the bay. From a new angle the same thing looks different and once they felt lost, I brought them back the same way we came.

The surface of the water was tight like new pudding. The sun was starting to fall off over the west and made long, green streaks in the water from the grass's reflection. Cranes and herons sat perched in trees and flew up in the air when we came and then settled back down on the twisted branches when we were gone.

We swerved back and forth around the bends and I leaned into the turns to keep ahead of the tour. The water line was up to the high banks and the grass waved and looked like you could almost walk across it and sit under the twisted marsh trees and watch the sun disappear. *Hell,* I thought, *even if you could, the bugs would come and carry you away.* It was hard to forget the bugs and their way of ruining special moments.

We passed a skiff at slow speed and watched them pull a stingray from the water. It wriggled on the hook and a boy pinned it against the boat with his foot to take the hook out while his father waved to us. I didn't want to leave the creek once I got into it. I never did. I could stay here all night, I thought, except for the bugs, but we had them in the apartment anyway. I wondered what day it was. Not that it mattered. In

Charleston, yesterday filled like a cup of water and when it was full it spilled into today until today was full and then that spilled into tomorrow until all the days spilled over and mixed into one. I could never remember which one we were in, except to know that by the time I pulled out of the creek I had been there so long the days were getting shorter and there were less tourists because of school.

In the late afternoon I took the boat out in the bay and watched as the water settled and the cool evening breeze began to blow in. The boat traffic slowed in the evening and it was quiet and clean like in the morning.

On the other end of the bay were the breakers from the sandbars and behind me lay the silent creek slowly flowing in to fill the marsh. I moved inland and rippled the water as I passed the dancing grass and nesting cranes. An osprey swooped down and took a fish from the creek and disappeared into a clump of old trees. I was alone and thought I'd rather have someone there to share it with. I cut the engine as a porpoise surfaced on the side of the boat and the quiet of the late summer air filled my ears and carried my breath. The evening air was sitting on the water and nothing was moving and there was no noise except for the patter of the porpoises surfacing and then sinking back under. After it was quiet, they got more playful until the water danced with them splashing and diving on all sides of the boat. They'd be eating soon and were playful and curious. I climbed down the ladder and dangled in the water as they splashed around me—one minute up, the next down.

"Will!" Jay's voice crackled loud over the radio and I jumped from the water and called back.

"What?"

"Hey, don't forget we're going out tonight."

"What time is it?"

"Almost six. We gotta pull these skis and get downtown."

Without a glance, I turned from the creek and headed back to the dock, leaving paradise and the quiet behind.

※

When we got to Harry's everyone was laughing and yelled their excitement when they saw us. The porch was full of girls—tan legs showing under short sundresses and running down to sandals and ending with painted toenails. They were drinking vodka tonics and the guys were drinking wine. Jay opened another bottle and talked to a girl I'd never seen before.

"I say," said Harry, fumbling with his cigarettes and poking Jack in the arm. "Got a light, boss?"

Jack handed him some matches and after more fumbling Harry began again.

"I say we go to the Boat House for dinner and then to the Blind Tiger for drinks on the patio."

"What about drinks before dinner?" asked a girl sitting on Cal's lap.

"We drink at the restaurant bar, then at the table and any place else that'll serve you drinks."

The restaurant bar wasn't much more than that and barely fit us at all. Jay smiled as he ordered vodka tonics for the girl I'd never seen before. Later that night he left with her and we all laughed when he said she was the one, but later on she still was.

Harry never talked, but yelled and pulled at my arm if I turned my head. We smoked cigarettes and drank wine. The bartender's eyes shot a fierce warning when Harry kicked a barstool and sent it skidding across the floor.

"What do you think, boss?" Harry said. He raised his eyebrows and pulled his hands across his new Hawaiian shirt.

"Nice, but I don't think the plaid shorts were the right call to go with it."

"Nah, love it. And the girls…they love it."

He started shuffling his feet and swaying his hips to his own music. The horror on the face of the woman sitting at the table facing us was made worse only when Cal joined in. He put his arm around Harry's waist and swayed with him.

"Easy, pal."

"Oh you love me, Harry."

"I think you're a fruitcake is what I think."

"Oh you gotta be kidding me," Cal said when he saw Jay and Jack coming over carrying shots for everyone.

"That's right," Jack said, handing us the tiny plastic cups. "Drink up."

I felt the bite of the alcohol tingle on my tongue and then felt the warm as it went down. The warm was in my stomach when I lost the room behind good friends. Two were laughing and two were dancing. I stood smiling and watched. Then, as we were heading to our table, Alex came in and ordered a drink for himself and something extra for each of us.

"I'm gonna have two of these before I order," said Harry, who never drove, pointing to his whiskey and water.

"Whiskey and soda?" asked the waiter innocently. We all turned our heads.

"No! No, it's a Jack Daniels with a little water. No soda. None. But an ashtray would be great."

"Why don't you make more noise, you prick?" Jack said to Harry when the waiter was gone.

"Cause, Jack—" Harry leaned back to bring us all in. "—this is our place. We drink here. We eat here. This is our place. If I get loud I do."

We all had small budgets, but spent money on little except food and drinks, so we ate out a lot and drank even more. That night we were drinking so much you couldn't reach anything on the table because of all the empty glasses. Harry told the waiter to clear them and we all ordered another. Then he lit a cigarette and stared adoringly at a quiet blond whose name I kept forgetting.

"Yeah, hey, so tell me," his words shot out in a quick and jumbled heap. "What is it you do here?"

"Work. At a law firm on East Bay."

Harry sat up. "How long?"

"Almost a year."

"Where'd you go to school?"

"I graduated from NYU and then law school at Boston University."

The conversation carried on for twenty minutes. Harry asked questions and gave philosophy and Anna—Anna was her name—kept pace and was passing with flying colors. I kept score in between jokes with Jack and Alex about other people in the restaurant. I thought she might make the cut when she fell hard.

"What are you reading?"

"Well, I usually only read magazines—*Cosmo*, *Time*—but there's a book from Oprah's book club that I bought. It's on the bestseller list. It's called *The Rightest Wrong*. Have you read it?"

We all got quiet except for Jay who was still talking to the girl with no name. Harry started in and I think Anna got pretty mad, but that was the idea. We never saw her again.

After we finished our drinks, Jack and Jay sprung for the bill like always and we went back downtown. The car doors creaked and slammed behind us as we stepped out onto Broad Street. We passed the old courthouse and the private firms and the church spires that marked the start of the south of Broad area. Harry walked in the street and was loud and funny. Jay talked quietly to the girl with no name. The leaning brick buildings were packed together and in the soft white light of the street lamps they were faded and genuine. We climbed the worn stairs to the Blind Tiger, the wood planks on the floor of the main room giving a little under our feet. Gas lamps threw a little light across the thick wooden tables and the brick walls as we passed through onto the terrace. Some nights Harry would get bored so he would call people he didn't like just to show them up. So he called Mason and we met him outside at a table with five faces I had seen before, but never tried to remember.

They all stood to shake hands and Mason gave a "'bout time," as Jack dragged a table across the slate patio and lined it up with theirs. The waiter was bringing drinks when Mason turned to me.

"Will. What's up?"

We shook hands and talked about the beach. He had been fishing that afternoon. After a minute we ran out of small talk.

"Yeah. Cool."

"Yeah. OK." He turned back to someone he had come with and they started talking and I sat down. We came from different worlds and I'd never understand the pickup truck culture he represented. I was still a Yankee and an outsider.

"Let's drink to the summer," said Jay as he stood up and winked at me. "And to new friends and to another year without the passage of time."

We drank and laughed and leaned back in our chairs. The waitress brought more drinks and we flirted with the girls who cheered when their songs came on and gave their own toasts. Theirs was another world I never belonged to and they never really belonged to ours. But they took pictures and we hung on their walls and when the better hours were gone, I suppose they remembered us.

Jay and the unnamed girl walked home at two in the morning and that was really where it all began.

"I have a toast of my own," said Harry who was normally less sentimental than Jay. "To Jay. To all of us." Then he paused and smiled and said, "To today and not because yesterday is so close, but because tomorrow is so far."

※

In the morning we woke up early and jumped in Jay's truck. We drove through downtown and across the long bridge over the bay through the marsh and past my favorite view. The view was uglier some mornings when my head hurt and when all the things that couldn't touch us in the guilt-free night knew their moment had come. The shrimp boats were sailing and as we started to hook up the trailer, Jack was coming back from the shop with food in his hands.

"Grease."

Jay and I jumped into his truck to drop the skis in the water. His face was tan and peeling under his stubble beard.

"Been two hours since I've been with her now."

That was all he said. It was enough. We ate cheese steaks and onion rings on the dock and drank orange soda. There were no morning tours and Jack stayed to take credit cards and send people out and Jay and I went to check on the half-dozen people who were on morning rides.

On the dock I'd washed down three aspirin with orange soda, but in the inlet, with the wind blowing and the waves chopping and water spraying and jet skis howling, my head pounded to the beat of last night's memories. I took off my life jacket and steered with my feet, reclining all the way back on the vinyl seat.

"Sky looks so angry," I said, lying on my back with my hands crossed behind my head. "With the clouds like that I mean. The way they're chasing each other around."

"The scorched breath of a clear morning." Jay looked at me and smiled and we laughed for a minute then got silent and looked back at the angry sky.

Jay was the first to break the silence.

"This summer was the end you know."

"Yeah."

"I knew things were going to change," he said. "The lines on the toilet at Willy's. Everything we've talked about for so long. This summer was the climax."

"The time never passed 'til today, you know."

"What do you mean?"

I said, "Just that the lines and the Bloodys and the jokes and the philosophy and Harry's poetry—they were all symptoms. Today marks the first definite point."

"Why's that, huh?"

"Been four hours since you've seen her now, Jay."

He smiled and splashed water at me with his hand.

"'Bout time, anyway." He laughed again and leaned back to look at the sky.

A thin, smeared cloud ran from the harsh breath of the sky as a dull thud sailed across the inlet, followed by the sound of a jet ski whining as it dipped below the water. From across the inlet I only saw four jet skis. To the east, a fifth spun in slow circles next to a small island. I saw a man swimming in the water towards bubbles marking where the sixth ski was sinking.

"Jay! Jay, get up!"

I raced across the inlet to what I thought was just an accident and then I saw the blood.

Two hours later I sat on an oyster-covered beach as tiny waves lapped on the shells, which clicked as they rubbed against the sand. The gentle buzz of a motor faded out the voices coming from the Coast Guard outboard across the creek. The man was strapped to a gurney, his neck held tight with white tape. I could look now because the blood was gone.

"You OK, Will?"

Jay pulled the boat alongside the island, stopping just far enough to keep from hitting bottom. I didn't answer.

"So, I'm gonna tow your jet ski back now. You think you wanna come?"

I eased my way across the oysters, careful not to step heavily on the sharp edges and waded into the water and climbed the ladder to the boat. He started as soon as I got in.

"Couldn't look. I mean, I didn't know what happened, but I couldn't look."

Jay had left when he saw the accident. He radioed for help from the creek and went back to lead the game warden to the wreck. I stayed at the accident sight. It looked brave later—me staying with the bleeding and broken man as he hung limp in his friend's arms. The truth was that I wanted to stay at a distance and got close only by mistake. I never saw the blood until I was close. Then it was too late.

"I waited by the jet skis," I said. "Fifteen feet away. I could hear him, though. Kept saying, 'Help me.' Every time he did teeth or skin or something came out of his mouth and plopped into the water. We couldn't help him. Hell, his friend was the only one close and he's the bastard who almost knocked his head off with that jet ski."

A fifteen-foot center console idled in the creek.

"How about that guy over there?" Jay asked.

"The guy in the boat? He's a doctor. The first one here. I think he radioed for the game warden too. He was calm the whole time." My lips quivered as I spoke.

"Not us."

"No. Not us."

"Whadd'ya think?"

"His friend hit him. Got too close and skipped across a wave. The doctor saw it all and said if that guy hadn't turned his head he would have lost it. The jet on the belly of the ski hit him. Took his skin, his jaw, his teeth." I shuddered and looked out at the water.

The game warden came to the dock later when we were pulling the broken skis from the water and asked us questions. He said the guy's name was Drew and his friend was David. Drew would need five days of reconstructive surgery to put his jaw back in place. David would need longer to put himself back together. The warden started to walk down the dock, then stopped and turned back.

"Those boys were stupid. Almost killed one another the way they were acting. Think they can just race around. Problem is they don't know they can't handle it 'til it's too late. You need somebody in court, you just call me, OK?"

"Yeah, thanks," said Jay.

I went to the dumpster to throw away the life jacket and some plastic from the ski. Marvin was leaning against the dumpster. I told him the story and he shook his head then focused his eyes on the life jacket.

"I'm 'a take the bloody jacket, if 'as OK." I nodded and gave it to him so he could clean it and sell it back to the marina. When I got back to the dock, Jay was closing at the register.

"I'm done, Jay." It was two in the afternoon.

"I am too. It's been a long day."

"No. I mean, I'm done."

He stopped and looked at me. Then he looked at the ground and then back at me.

"I know. Come on, I'll give you a ride to Harry's."

※

Jay's cell phone was the first sound I heard over the hum of his truck rumbling across the connector. He grabbed it from the console and held it to his mouth.

"Yeah! No, we're leaving. I don't really wanna get into it. Here." He pushed the phone to me without looking.

"Yeah? Hey. No. We're leaving. 'Cause. I don't really wanna talk about it. Hold on. Jay, you wanna meet them at the beach? Folley?"

"No. But I'll drop you off."

Going to Folley meant crossing almost a half-dozen more bridges. Going anywhere in Charleston did. We crossed them all and at the end of the last was a sign that read: "Folley Beach—The edge of America." We passed it without a word. We passed the old shrimp boats and the splintered marsh grass and dirt driveways and made a left at the only major intersection in the area. Jay pulled the car up alongside the rocks that lined the road and separated it from the dunes.

"I know why you're leaving. And it's cool."

"I know." I didn't look up at him. I got out of the car and crossed the plank bridge and pulled my shirt off over my head and jumped in the water. Jay's truck was gone when I stood up. He was off to see the anonymous girl.

The air at the beach was thick and hot and my skin stung as the salt dried in the sun, but Harry had two fifths of Jim Beam and we mixed it with Coke in plastic cups. I told him about the accident.

"See, that's bullshit," he said. "People are stupid and they don't pay attention to what's going on until it's too late. What time is it?"

"Three."

"Man, I'm drunk. Blind drunk."

"Me too." I took another drink.

There were no girls with us. It was just us and some vacationing families who increased the divide between our towels and theirs more and more as we drank Jim Beam and laughed out loud and ran waist-deep into the water to pee. By half past three my face was warm and my head was fuzzy. Liquor always muffles voices and I spoke louder. We all did.

The plastic seal from the second fifth was tight and I cut my hand trying to break it off and blood ran down my arm like rain on a windshield. I shook it viciously and turned back to the bottle. Tiny specks of blood splattered on my chest and face. I didn't notice. I turned to Alex and handed him a cup.

"Where the hell is everyone going?" I asked.

Alex pointed to a beach house across the road. It was blue with gray trim and with sandy stairs leading up to the door. Cinder blocks surrounded by bamboo trees were stacked in five columns that lifted the house fifteen feet off the lawn to keep it from being washed away by hurricanes. "To go to the bathroom, I guess."

Using the ocean gets tiresome, even if it is easier and I followed them and we walked into the shaded area under the house and used the bushes or stood behind the pillars. The shade felt good on my back and shoulders, like a drink, and I pushed my forehead against the cold blocks. I closed my eyes and the beach was gone and so was the sun and the sticky salt and there was only the cold of the blocks and the warm of the liquor.

"Christ, Will. What the hell happened to you?" asked Jack, bleary-eyed and swaying back and forth.

"I don't know. Why?"

"You got blood all over yourself." He turned back to the bushes and I closed my eyes and leaned against the pillar and he started talking to a surfer about the waves and the wind and he knew nothing about either and he didn't know the surfer.

The second fifth was gone by quarter past four. Cal and Alex walked out on the jetties and tried to push each other off and Jack and Harry floated in the water. I sat on the beach and spun. The waves rocked back and forth until I couldn't watch. I lay back on the sand in the deep footprints and the holes that the little kids dig. On my back the sky spun too, but it never rocked. Nervous parents turned their children from me. I was on the verge of passing out when the yelling started.

"I said shut up. Just shut your friggin' mouth."

My head started spinning again when I looked up. I tried too hard to focus bleary eyes on the four figures in front of me and only got dizzy. Through the spinning I could see Jack and Cal fighting on the sand. I watched them push each other back and forth and I walked on stiff legs across the bumpy sand and pulled on Jack's arm but he swung it and I fell back. The breath bumped out of my lungs as I landed flat on my back and my stomach tightened and I knew that it would happen. *Well, that's it*, I thought. You never know when you've had too much until after you've had it and even then sometimes it takes something to pull it along.

I was too drunk to see what was happening but I could hear it. I could hear Jack and Cal and Harry and Alex and someone else and the surfers were yelling and a strange man's voice screaming and I thought it was the father whose children had been digging holes. *Good*, I thought, *I've been falling in your damn holes all day*. Then I heard the waves and car doors and then someone standing over me and I opened my eyes. The sun was sharp and I closed them, but it was too late and my head was spinning and my stomach made one last fall.

"We gotta go. Pack your shit," said someone over me and I rolled onto my face and pulled my hands and knees under me and then stood.

My towel was moving faster than I was and when I bent down to pick it up I missed and did a belly flop on the packed sand. Fifteen wobbly steps from the rocks was almost too many, but I made it in time. Another mother grabbed her children and took them to the car. We had been drunk and loud and had gone to the bathroom in someone's lawn and in the water and now we were fighting and I was getting sick. The mother's car door slammed as Alex grabbed the back of my bathing suit and pulled me away.

Harry and Jack argued and Cal panted furious breaths, his fists clenched. I was still looking through a murky kaleidoscope. Then Jack was gone. Cal packed in silence and Alex dragged me toward the car.

"I got two words for you," Harry slurred. "Peaking Too Early."

Cal dropped us off at Harry's apartment and pulled out of the driveway. I opened the door and walked down the driveway with my eyes half-open and heard the car pull away.

❦

I woke up at 10:30 and Harry was on the porch drinking and watching the fireflies zip across and back. I sat on the edge of the porch and he asked if I wanted to know what happened and I said that I knew enough about why so what wasn't really the question. He walked inside and came out with two drinks in his hands.

"I'm leaving tomorrow. I got a letter from my sister. She's in Atlanta," I said.

"I'll come with you."

"Why?"

"To get away from here. To get lost."

"You know it's the same as here. Maybe worse."

"I'm leaving either way. You want to ride the Dog alone or with me?"

We argued it for a while before I let up. Then we just drank beer on the porch and wondered what everyone would do when we were gone.

"Jay will be married in a year, I bet."

"Cal's getting a job. Back home. Alex will stay," Harry said.

"Jack?"

"I don't know. He'll be OK. They all will. Time will pass and this place will still be here when we're gone. But we'll remember some of it." He paused. "It was more than the booze today. You know that, right?"

"Yeah, I think I always have," I said.

We got drunk off of Palmettos for the last time and I looked through the palms and across the street.

"You know it'll be over tomorrow when we wake up."

"It'll be over tomorrow or it won't." Harry walked back inside and went to bed.

When I woke up, the apartment was quiet. Cars passed in the street, but inside it was still. Two empty liquor bottles on the counter were the only evidence that it had been what it had been. I let out a long breath and then showered and dressed. Harry came downstairs with a bag and we walked out.

Book II

Green trees packed with fat leaves crowded the highways from Charleston to Atlanta. The vibrant undergrowth of the South came to life as the bus carried us inland. A man with tobacco-stained fingers and an old green jacket sat across from me, repeating song lines in a quiet voice.

A haze hovered ahead as we approached the city with its smog ceiling and silhouetted mountains silent and gray. Atlanta is alive with movement. It's alive from the dirty secrets of Underground to the dirtier ones further north. Cars crisscross the crowded streets. Buildings reach up at sporadic intervals and urban sprawl bites into fashionable neighborhoods. The city is dirty and crowded and sometimes ugly and cold, but it's alive. Thick trees, wrapped in brown and green vines, surrounded by bushes crammed together like MARTA riders, line the perimeter and run across the North Georgia landscape and into the heights of Appalachia. Streams cut banks, steep and jagged with rocks, into sub-tropical forests tall with ancient trees.

History books outline Sherman's much maligned capture of Atlanta and the burning of the city, the destruction of its plantations and paper mills and centers. But what Sherman stole was the heart of Atlanta and what remains is a shell, void of character and history. It was 3:30 when we reached Atlanta. And it was hot.

"Tell me, boss. What's the story with your sister?"

"She's my sister. Haven't seen her in a few years."

"She know we're coming?"

"Me. Not you."

"What's she gonna say?"

"To you? Probably tell you get the hell out."

"Yeah, real friggin' funny."

We met my sister at a MARTA station downtown. Her brown eyes winked a fake smile through black rings. I hugged her and patted my hands on bones close to the skin and almost visible through her shirt. She wiped a sweaty hand on her faded jeans before shaking Harry's and pulled a cigarette from her pocket.

"Oh, here—I got it." Harry fished for his lighter. His arm swung as he struck the flint and cursed the sparks. Penny took a match from her pocket and lit her cigarette. Harry got the lighter going and pushed it toward her face.

"Thanks." She turned without looking, stepped onto the escalator, and drummed her fingers on the railing as she glided out of sight.

Atlanta's eastside is, in essence, a recovering addict. Old buildings were repainted and dirty carpets pulled. New and younger tenants fill the rented units lining the streets and the grassy parks and the coffee shops and the tiny restaurants, but the underbelly remains the same. Less than a decade before us, visitors never strayed into the eastside. Too many shootings, robberies, and drugs. An early '90s citywide movement to reclaim Atlanta's downtown brought cash to the neighborhood and a revitalized image for squatters like us who never knew the difference. Not much was changed, really. Penny's place was old and the walls were hollow. Hookers stomped across the streets in the dark hours and homeless men in the day. Once an addict, always an addict.

We followed Penny up the escalator and stepped out into the honking and yelling street swirling with cars and people.

"I'm going to Zestos for lunch. If you two wanna come they have a fish sandwich special on Fridays."

The streets and sidewalks in Atlanta were dirty with papers and filled with people and reminded me of the ones I had grown up on. Harry, too, was more alive in the bigger city, more at home where his antics weren't so conspicuous.

We ate lunch and laughed at old stories and told new ones about Charleston and about Texas, where Penny had been living. She was divorced. Her husband calmed her wild voice when they were young only to find three years later that she was not really tamed at all. She still wanted to travel. Her wandering eyes grew tired and dim in the security-conscious world of claustrophobia. She tried her hand at writing. The family trait of exaggeration ran more rampant than our name and she banged out page after page about a restless childhood and ironclad dreamboats. But I saw little of the young girl I had whipped with a ski pole on Christmas morning, and cigarettes had hardened the tender voice that chased away twelve years worth of midnight monsters.

"And you quit your job and took a bus south." Penny's electric smile came back and I knew I was home. "You have to understand, Harry, that the last time I saw him, he was in high school pretending to love my Led Zepplin records and calling seventeen-year-old girls."

Harry leaned back in his chair and laughed. I looked into Penny's eyes and she coiled back.

"Yeah, well, I'm not sniffing my money these days and the writing has taken off." She was playing with her hands and looking at someone in the street.

"Mom never read it," I said. "She won't."

Penny laughed through thinly tearing eyes. "Not *Good Housekeeping*, but it pays the bills. Anyone wanna drink? Let's go to the Highlands."

Virginia Highlands borders downtown Atlanta and offers the only real break from the more turbulent Buckhead. Highlands is dotted with parks and converted old houses and the dirty grocery stores are giving way to new, clean shopping centers. Some parts are ugly and dark, but it's a good look at urban life, complete with hole-in-the-wall restaurants and shopping cart-clogged alleys. We had drinks in a Mexican restaurant and ate cheese queso and chili rellenos and smoked cigarettes.

"I love a nice soft buzz in the afternoon." Harry's face was red like Penny's and mine was warm and probably red too. "So the question, Penny, is can you get a couple of hack writers something to buy drinks with?"

Penny said that her friends were putting together a restaurant review.

Harry smiled. "Well, I eat. Suppose I can write about it." Then he stood and waved his arm frantically at the waiter. "Yo!

Señor! Bring us another pitcher of margaritas and make them strong. We're writing a review."

⁂

At eight we went to Penny's place in East Atlanta. The stairs to the second floor were wooden and old and creaked under the weight of six feet. Penny twisted the key from side to side the way you have to on old latch locks and pushed the door open. I wiped my shoes on the straw mat and walked across the apartment. Our voices and the creak of the floorboards echoed off the close facing walls. I washed my face in her bathroom sink, which groaned and shuttered when water came out and sat on the edge of the claw-foot tub that crowded the room. Penny was still talking.

"All I have is a couch, but it pulls out and you can use it," she said, her back against a bookshelf that ran the length of the main room. "The French doors open, so go outside if you wanna smoke. The railing is loose, though, so don't lean against it unless you wanna meet the guys downstairs."

"So, you gonna cook us food and everything?" Harry was trying to break Penny into his humor. She was breaking him into hers as well.

"Sure. Eggrolls." She laughed and her eyes shined. The last time she made egg rolls I was in the seventh grade. She broke a glass and a piece of it landed in the mix and I bit into it and cut my mouth. We talked until three—Penny comes alive after midnight—and I slept well despite the moans of an old building.

East Atlanta was a short ride from the business district that housed the offices of Atlanta's newest restaurant review. Penny worked from her house now, writing from seven until noon, napping and then writing again. She lent us her car with stern warnings. I looked out the window as I drove and watched the people walking and talking and napping on the sidewalks and in the doorways. It was hotter than Charleston because there was no ocean breeze. Only asphalt. The sun and the heat radiated from the streets and burned your feet through your shoes. Along the way, we watched men sitting on stoops with wet towels around their necks and women fanning themselves from second-story windows. Once downtown, I parked the car in a lot and the ticket taker, an Indian man sheltered from the sweltering heat by only a small tin booth and a six-inch oscillating fan, directed us to the building.

We rode the elevator, which was more like a freight elevator, and you had to pull the iron gate shut and lock the inner door with a giant steel lever. We got out and walked across the lobby and through the double wooden doors and into the main office. We met the editor, Michelle, who was our age and spoke with a thick Southern accent. Her face was marked with the same signs as Penny's. She told us we were supposed to eat at as many restaurants as we could in Fulton County and write a 250-word review for them. The salesmen, who wore black pants and black shirts and silver belt buckles, sold the ads that paid our salaries. They sold to restaurants and part of our job was to look favorably on those that bought them. It was underhanded, but we were broke.

"When, uh, can you guys start?"

"Today, really. I ate Mexican last night and woke up with the shits. I got a few choice words for that place." Harry was serious, but he was laughing because it was funny and also because Michelle was serious about being an editor, and he knew he was better than she was.

"Well, I'd love you to start today, but—," she breathed deep, "—if you could leave out the part about the—."

"The shits? Yeah, sure, but it would have made great copy. You got a bathroom in this joint?"

I think Michelle called my sister as soon as we left to make sure we were reliable. Penny lied and we got the job.

France measures all distances from point zero in Paris. Peachtree Street serves a similar function for Atlanta, with Peachtree streets crisscrossing and swerving around the city and making too many appearances to make any sense. The *Review* occupied the eleventh floor of the flatiron building on the corner of Peachtree and Peachtree in the Fairlie Poplar District, which ran several blocks in each direction. Harry and I usually ate lunch at a strip of small restaurants facing sidewalks painted with Poplar trees and picnic tables. Most of the buildings are three stories and fashioned in 1950s architecture with old ads for tobacco and candy peeling off the brick walls. Students, living in tiny one-room studios, and the trendy twenty-somethings like the ones at the *Review* who live in high-dollar lofts, fill the district. Penny had friends there who never fit in with the ad salesmen. They met at the cafés in the afternoon and the first time I went there I walked alone.

Their favorite spot was the Fairlie Poplar Café. It was a one-room Moroccan café, with a bar running along one wall. We sat at tables against the far brick wall and pulled chairs all around, which never bothered the waiters because the room was open and the tables were spread apart. We drank wine and gimlets and talked about politics and people, but never anything serious and touchy. The waiters loved to give their special hot sauce to trusting customers to watch them choke on the heat.

The café is a block from Peachtree Street with alleys on either side. I left the *Review* and passed parking garages and service entrances and the back side of the Circuit Court. Nobody ever used the back street for walking except the homeless who slept on mashed boxes behind walls that blocked the wind. It was bad when I first got there because I never knew what to say when they begged me. Ignore them or be an enabler. I didn't know where I stood so the first few times they found me I got nervous and jumpy. It figures that the first guy who approached me was pushy and he scared me off the back streets for weeks.

"I'm sick of this shit, man. I hate it." The guy was screaming. Standing behind the library, scratching his nappy hair and pulling on his layers of coats as he stomped his feet on the sidewalk. "Hate this, man. I hate it." When he saw me coming down the sidewalk he locked on like a salesman. "Hey, man. You got a dollar?"

"Sorry, but I don't carry cash." It was true, but he'd heard it before.

"Fifty cents? Anything?"

I shook my head.

"You lost? Where you going?"

I pointed to the café.

"Hell, you lost? Let me help you."

"Not lost. I'm going right there."

"Where? You lost? Where you tryin' to go?" He crossed the street and was walking a few steps behind me. Defensiveness was warming my face.

"I'm not lost. Sorry." I kept walking and he turned and started yelling into the air again. Penny always laughed at me because once they didn't scare me I stopped to talk to them or paid for their booklets and once had my portrait done by a man in a cigarette-burned sweater. They were considered a burden, but I liked them. I liked the way they broke up the day and that some of them didn't care about us and ignored us more than we ignored them.

I can't say that I really remember much about meeting Penny's friends. Some were students in their late twenties who did nothing and others worked odd jobs to pay the bills and really worked at night. Penny was close with a guy named Oren and she pretended they were only friends but we all knew it was more. He was a student and a front man for a local band and so he had dyed his hair orange, but when it washed out it never went back to blonde. Most of their friends were former dreamers who spent time in Colorado or Southern California and had come back home to work and were certain I'd do the same.

"Give yourself a few years," one girl said. "You'll run away then get tired of doing nothing and you'll come back to get a job." She smiled at her logic and it made her happy to think that if she never did it, it couldn't be done.

Penny ignored most of what was said and talked to Oren and when she wasn't ignoring me, she was calling me out.

"So you have a job, now. What are you gonna do?"

"Gee, Penny. I hadn't really thought about it. Maybe live with you for a year or two."

"That's funny. Really." Penny's second book was on the horizon, but it wasn't what she wanted to write and she was bitter. "It's so damn hard to let go." It was five in the afternoon. We sat there eating grilled chicken sandwiches topped with the special hot sauce and got drunk until we couldn't see the street. When the ringing in my ears was louder than the talk, I paid my tab and hopped MARTA back to Penny's and slept the day off.

Harry fell asleep in a chair so he got up early the next morning and walked to the couch and pulled the pillow out from under my head.

"You got a review, boss?" His voice was fresh and bounced off the walls as he paced the room.

"No." My mouth was fuzzy and my head was still aching. "What time is it?"

"Eight. Get up. We gotta eat."

"I went to Fairlie Poplar Café yesterday. I'll use that."

"That's great. Now get off your ass and come with me to a restaurant."

Penny was sitting on her bed writing when we left. She hadn't slept in two days. At least, not in her own bed. We ate at a filthy diner with runny eggs and bad coffee and bad waitresses. Ours scolded me when I asked for a Bloody Mary and Harry was set to write a bad review when Michelle told him that they were advertisers. It was changed to omit the runny eggs and recommend the waffles.

Sleeping Dogs

Southeast summers are not tolerable even by local standards and the general practice is to move from building to car and back again without sweating too heavily. Atlanta employs a force of ambassadors—complete with safari hats, shorts, and button-down khaki shirts—to answer questions and assist travelers. Curious or lost visitors, however, would have to walk through dirty streets into air-conditioned buildings where wheezing ambassadors spend their afternoons talking with receptionists and security guards in the lobbies of hotels and office complexes. They were handy paradoxes and, mixed in with bitter public workers and the anxious business class, provided fodder for a memoir that Harry spent his days writing.

Penny's friends spent the afternoons in the café. I was drunk by ten, mixing gimlets with Oren in open protest to the ready-made world of globalization.

"Suburbs, Will. Suburbs were made by a generation that had seen hard times and were ready to relax." Oren and I were drunk before noon almost every day. "Security is great if you've known something else, but what if you haven't? Like us? You gotta make it tough yourself. You have to survive before you can live."

If Atlanta was alive, so were we. We were artists, though we spent more time in the café than we did making art. That was our rebellion, our pathway to less worn pathways. We drank our way through, and when that wasn't enough we sniffed it.

"You don't need to move to California and get rid of your stuff. Live here and create and do what you want. Break their rules on their turf." He laughed. "I always wanted to find a place to use the word turf."

It was clearly open rebellion.

When I got home, I fell asleep on the couch. I was waking my generation through good example. Harry stayed up and typed his memoirs.

The afternoon heat was unfit for sobriety and the evening was little consolation. When the sun dipped down behind the green hills to the west, the sticky air changed little. The orange tint of midday gave way to the blue tint of the moon and artificial lighting, but your clothes still clung to your back.

I napped from four until seven, showered, dressed, and punched a 250-word review out on Penny's processor and gave it to Harry to fax to the *Review*. We'd mix drinks from eight until nine, then drive across town or ride MARTA to a restaurant where we had reservations for three or four.

"I'm sick of Buckhead. We're not going to Buckhead, are we?" Penny was simple when we were children and fashion did little to change her opinion.

Buckhead was full of restaurants with dress codes and high-priced wines and men with shaved heads wearing black suit jackets with black shirts that had no collars. The walls were decorated with Warhol reprints or black and white cityscapes and the cigar lounges and waiting areas were hung with pictures of celebrities sharing a martini with the owners. People we knew went there to wear shocking clothes and act scandalous and show they weren't part of the crowd.

"No, I got us reservations outside of the perimeter."

"So we have to drive?"

"Unless you plan on taking the bus." Harry still thought he was funny.

"Outside of the perimeter?" The perimeter is a circular highway surrounding the heart of metro Atlanta. If you lived inside, as a rule you never left. Life was boring out there—in the woods. Some of the people who lived outside never went inside after dark, but that was because they feared a rising crime rate.

"Yup," he said.

"OK, OK. It's outside the perimeter," I said. "I think we'll live." Their arguments switched from polite dissention to openly vicious, like a failing marriage, and I played the unfavorable role of appeasing child. "I'll drive. Let's go."

The car casually dripped water from the overused air conditioner as we walked across the parking lot to the last building in the tiny strip mall squeezed next to a Red Lobster and Bank of America. Our reservations were at the House of Chan. Nobody had been there. Harry heard about it from someone else and thought it sounded good and here we were. We pushed through a plastic-covered porch with heaters in the corner to keep it warm on winter nights and walked through the front door and into the tiny waiting area.

"Is three?" said a skinny man with short black hair and a red sweater vest.

"Yes."

"OK, three menu and right this—."

"No, no! They wait." A woman standing behind the register pushed him aside with one hand while swiping credit cards with the other.

"Oh, sorry. We have wait. Name?"

"Harry. H-A—"

"Oh, AJ. OK, AJ. You wait, OK?"

The restaurant was no bigger than the smoking section of any restaurant in the perimeter. The waiters wove through narrow lanes between crowded tables and the waiting line occasionally strung out the door. Restaurant reviews, some from as early as 1985, were hung next to more reviews and praised House of Chan as the best Chinese restaurant in Atlanta.

"We gotta get this place if we wanna make the big time." Harry was joking, but only because he never planned on making it big as a restaurant critic. He wrote a great review before we sat down and it later hung on the wall.

The House became our favorite and we ate there more than twice a week. AJ, party of three. We drank Tsingtao beer from the fat green bottle and ordered Mongolian beef or Peking duck and sipped oriental tea from tiny ceramic cups without handles.

℘

I met Oren for drinks on a Thursday morning. September was nearly through, but the leaves had not yet begun to change. It was still too hot. I sat on the dirty, plastic bench seats of the train and read a newspaper. The peace talks were floundering and violence had taken their place. The election was going full-steam. I was drunk or high. The world was moving without me.

"I gotta run to the bank and get cash." Oren was always short on cash because he thought that he would spend any money in his wallet. So he kept only about twenty dollars at a time and going to the bank got to be a chore.

The SunTrust bank was nestled in the middle of Peachtree Plaza, facing a courtyard with flags from more than a dozen countries. They represented a vain attempt to convey a feeling of international collaboration more than they did the nations from which they originated. Inside a man with a longshoreman cap and a white thermal undershirt with the sleeves rolled up was talking to a man ahead of him in line. The second man paid no mind to the conversation. The discussion spilled from the line to the counter while both men made transactions. As the longshoreman stuffed his wallet in his back pocket and moved toward the door, he turned to his unwilling accomplice and closed the discussion.

"Christ may have been a Roman or maybe even a Jew—hell he might have been a lot of things—but he wasn't a Negro," he shouted and walked out the door. He left a moment too soon to hear the laughter.

"That guy," said a black man in front of us, "did he look black to anyone else in here?"

Everyone laughed and nodded. He might've just been crazy or maybe he just never noticed, but he was black. His skin was pale like an albino, but his features and hair were definitely not white. We stood around and rolled our eyes and murmured to each other, then turned back to our lives and slipped out of each other's.

We ate an early lunch at the 5000 Deli, a small, family-operated grease pit that faced a side street and shouldered an alley behind the Winecoff Hotel.

With a mouth full of Reuben and onion rings, Oren started in. "Thing I try to do, Will, is I try to find that little piece of irony in every situation. Makes me happy." We were both cynical, but for different reasons. "Like my friend Janice. You've seen her, right?" He held his hands out in front of him to show how big her breasts were. "She always has bad relationships. And I don't think she just can't get away from bad guys. It's like she looks for them."

"Does it really matter?"

"Yeah." He continued and sometimes got boring and I blocked him out. "People view themselves a certain way. You know, how they want to be seen. But it's not always true. Because it's like people always change for each other. You know? To create their own reality."

I slipped off into thought and came back as he was finishing.

"It's just like, the answer is there all the time. But it's gotta rattle around in your head for a while. I don't know."

We walked outside and followed the sidewalk to the café. He continued about facades and reality and kicked his expensive boots along the curb. I thought about his parents. His mother loved the name Oren Alex, but his father's last name was Alexander. She named him anyway and his certificate read Oren Alexander Alexander.

Harry and Penny were in the café when we arrived, eating bread and drinking wine. I ordered a second bottle for the table and Oren's friend Janice came in the door. She had long legs covered in black pants and straight hair that rested below her shoulder blades. Harry had his notebook on the table and Penny was flipping through the pages.

"You always carry that?" Janice's voice was marked by the cutting accent of old Atlanta.

"Yeah." Harry filled my glass and didn't look up.

"Why?"

"Rust never sleeps."

"Do you ever use any of your own lines?"

"Some of the greatest words we'll ever read have already been written."

"Who said that?"
"Harold Metropole."
"Who's that?"
"A great writer."
"I've never heard of him."
"You will."

Janice squinted her eyes and turned the conversation. She had no time for unknown writers. There were too many fashionable films to watch by unknown filmmakers.

℘

In early October I met Delia Rothberg, a born Southern Baptist and practicing Jew. She converted secretly and unceremoniously while living in Manhattan. In New York she became a Jew by the composition of her name. What did it matter if the circumstances of her birth didn't dictate her inherent tendency toward Judaism? Jew or Christian, she was a friend of Harry's and he moved into her small apartment, which made life at Penny's easier.

Delia might have been a great writer, and we may never know, but she spent her time coaching Harry. They drank wine and ate avocados with Penny, who was editing the first draft of Harry's memoirs, now nearly eighty pages. They were already working by the time I came home drunk and when I woke up at seven they were finished and ready to go out for the night.

"Let's go to World Bar tonight. I feel like dancing." Delia always felt like dancing and sometimes we agreed and went along.

I started mixing drinks. "Harry, you want a gimlet?"

"No, I'm not drinking this week. I wanna see how it'll effect my writing."

"I never drink when I write. I've done drugs, but I didn't drink at all when I was writing my first book," said Penny.

"You're doing drugs now." Hangovers need a crowd and I was defensive.

"Not like I was. Anyway, shut up. You and Oren are doing more than anybody." Penny was feisty—like when we were children—and I loved to play along, but my head hurt and I felt sick so I just poured a drink and dropped on the couch.

When the clock chimes rang midnight I woke and raised my head. It was heavy and aching and my stomach was tight and my tongue was swollen. Everyone was gone. My first gimlet was on the coffee table. The ice was melted and the napkin was wet. I poured the drink out in the sink and made the bed. I faintly remember hearing Harry's scratchy voice in the night and when I woke around noon the next day they were all gone.

℘

October rolled on like a wagon racing down a paved hill and I was there, screaming like a child who realized at last that you can't control it with the tiny black handle, even if it is a Radio Flyer. A few days before Halloween I dodged Oren's calls and suffered through a morning hangover and was sober by two. There was a restaurant in Sandy Springs, Il Forno, that had New York-style food and a hole-in-the-wall atmosphere. A good review in untested waters would go a long way in salvaging the part-time job my negligence had nearly lost.

I ate a meatball sandwich on chewy bread and skipped the large beer selection in favor of a Coke. Wind swept across the gravel parking lot and pushed the plastic-flapped walls of the porch in and out while I ate. The guy behind the counter was amiable and I wrote a good review from the picnic table with its commanding view of the back of a roadside motel.

The motel was on the corner of Roswell Road and I-285 and it was the permanent residence of a healthy chunk of Atlanta's Mexican population. It was more like the way I always imagined Tijuana than Sandy Springs. Laundry hung from railings, and boxes, bicycles, and toys cluttered the balcony walkways. After lunch, I walked through the loose gravel lot to a gas station to buy a soda and some cigarettes. Eleven Mexican men, probably ranging from eighteen to at least forty, leaned against a four-foot concrete wall or sat on the ground, talking and smoking cigarettes. I sat on the wall next to a man in his mid-twenties and lit a cigarette. He asked me for a light. His name was Juan.

Juan was born in Mexico but immigrated to the States when he was nine with his father to find work. They worked in "bad places" with little pay and no insurance, but it was more than they made in Mexico so they stayed. Then they came to Atlanta and were supposed to find permanent landscaping jobs but with no green card he had to wait here instead.

"We get picked up by landscapers and stuff, you know? Nothing for real. Just one day at a time. I send some home and keep enough to live here." He jerked his thumb toward the hotel.

Juan had brothers that came to Atlanta in the back of a hay truck. The younger two lived with their grandfather and went by American names and were only allowed to speak English. They had green cards and one of them was in school. Juan never had that choice so he stayed here illegally and worked at bad places. I wasn't sure, nor am I sure, that I agreed with the way they got here. And I'm not sure that mattered. The dozen or so day laborers who came to the gas station waiting to get picked up in the morning were a decidedly inconspicuous fixture as far as native Atlantans were concerned. They sat cross-legged in the back of pickups, four or five at a time, and worked outside and were quiet. Landscapers and builders loved them because they'd work hard and ask for little besides a paycheck in return. I asked Juan what he wanted to do. He shook his head.

"Don't matter. Who cares? I have a family and they need money."

"Then what?"

"Huh?"

"After that?"

"There is no 'after that.' Only today and what money I get now," he said.

"You're not working now."

"Today was a better day once. Now nothing. But today will get better again. Later."

"When? Tomorrow?"

"No tomorrow. Just today and money and later."

※

Years and age have scattered the memory of most days of my youth like pine straw across the asphalt, with little remaining aside from occasional highlights of major mistakes or accomplishments. But Halloween still has a magical taste. I can smell the plastic from my mask and cape. I can see the cardboard box with the plastic see-through top from Woolworth where we bought it. The smell of logs burning and the faint rumblings of ghosts and witches, all alive and ready in the cemetery behind our two-story house, are as strong today as when I was twelve.

Naturally, then, when I awoke on Halloween, it was earlier than my traditional noon wake up and Penny and I sipped black coffee and talked about our long-ago life on VanBuren Avenue. It was one of the last hot days of the year. Delia and Harry came in at half past ten.

"What're you doin' up?" Delia was jealous of any time that Harry and I spent together and encouraged my daily alcohol binges.

"Shut up."

"Oh, will both of you shut the hell up? Christ, it's like living with animals." Harry had a way of being intolerant of any disturbances he had no part in creating. "Anyway, Al Gore is speaking today. I don't like him, but he's here and we might go and see him. You kids coming?"

We rode MARTA to the Peachtree station near Centennial Park and walked the last five blocks with the sounds of Lieberman pumping through the air. When we passed the Tabernacle we could hear the cheers of the crowd get louder as Al stepped up. It was hot. We crossed the street and reached the gates of the park. The crowd got heavy and was sweating and we decided to stay in the street where there was enough room to avoid rubbing against everyone's sticky wet arms.

"HELLO ATLANTA!" The crowd roared back a greeting. "Been a while, but I'm back." On the big screen television next to the stage I could see that Al was sweating through his white shirt. His tie was off and tucked into his pocket.

We pushed past people waiting in line to get in and people climbing on the fence to get a better view. Nobody dared jump over. Secret Service officers with radios and black vests talked into radios and swarmed like piranha.

I turned from Al and watched protestors with signs decrying the death penalty and the WTO and yelling that Gore and Bush were just two sides of one corporate head. More poured from vans parked across the street. They mixed with news crews and tried to draw attention. A middle-aged couple sat their daughter on a bucket with a sign in her hand. Her face was red and sweaty. She caught her mom's attention for a minute.

"I wanna go home. I'm hot." Mom smiled and patted her head.

Al continued, elevated by the applause of the middle class. He was talking about helping the working man. Saving the unions. A three-man construction crew picked at the road surrounding the park and never heard what he had to say over the jackhammer.

A group of pigeons picked at a boxed lunch that had been discarded next to the fence. One of them was small and had a gimped foot and he pecked at gravel and trailed the others who were eating well off the bread on the road. I stared at the bird, listening to the howl of the vice president answering his own rhetorical questions. A third-party candidate walked by and handed me a flyer. Harry spun around and hit my arm.

"What's up? You ready to eat?"

Penny, Harry, and Delia met Oren and Janice and some other people and went to a Halloween party at a bar in Buckhead. I stayed home and flipped through the channels. I thought about how I spent the previous Halloween with friends from school, back before my job got to be as intolerable as I was. Anyway, I wasn't in the mood to be happy.

*

The first time that I met one of Penny's boyfriends I was in the fifth grade. His name was Greg and he went to private school and he took her to a formal. My mom took pictures. He pinned a small, pink flower on her dress. I stood on the stairs with my friend Ryan and we laughed at how small Greg's legs looked. His tux had tails and the jacket hung low and to the eyes of a ten-year-old, he had short legs.

Penny broke up with Greg coldly and unexpectedly a week later and began dating his best friend. Two years later a mutual friend told her that Greg had since changed teams and that he, too, was in search of a new man. Fourteen years after first seeing someone actually willing to kiss my sister, I pulled the collar on my wool coat up around my neck and crossed the parking lot at the Windsor Estates.

"What the hell's his room number again?" Oren was as surprised by the news of Penny's new boyfriend as we were, but he took it harder.

"It's 2193. What's wrong, Oren? You're tense." Harry enjoyed the moment.

"Huh? Nothin'."

The concierge met us at the door.

"May I help you?"

"Yeah—2193, please. Rigsbey."

"Thank you." He called the room and turned back and waved us to the elevator. A doorman punched the second-floor button.

"Isn't this where Elton John lives?" Harry leaned against the wall, almost touching the doorman.

"Uh, sorry, but I can't tell you that." He inched toward the door.

"Don't you just love him? Daniel, you, yes you," Harry pointed his little finger toward the doorman, "are my brother."

"Ooo, ooo—I like Saturday night's alright for fighting." I said.

"Baaaaallerina."

The door opened and we piled out. Harry smirked at the doorman who was searching for something in his pocket and mashing the DOOR CLOSE key.

Twenty-one ninety-three was a door. A number on a door and it lacked pretense and judgment. What it represented, however, was one of the most expensive apartments in midtown—the trendiest neighborhood of all for the self-proclaimed young professionals. Jackson Rigsbey yanked the door open after my third bang—each painfully dull and solitary, like the ringing of a gong. Penny was in the kitchen, spearing olives for a martini.

"I'm Jackson. You must be Will."

"Lightfoot. Will Lightfoot. Restaurant critic."

"Yeah, yeah and let's not forget sometime wino. Let us in." Harry rushed past us and walked inside.

Oren crept in last. He and I had gone and gotten high before we left so I was nothing but energy. For Oren it only amplified how uncomfortable he felt and he stood behind us fidgeting.

Jackson followed us in, shuffling across hardwood floors into the gray-tiled kitchen. I held my hand up for Penny to high five, a perfectly respectable move for a younger brother trying to embarrass his older sister in front of a boy and show off for his friends.

"Quit." She was in no mood and sat down on a brown leather couch facing tall windows that looked out onto Piedmont Park.

"Oh this is great, you can see Piedmont. Isn't that where the gay guys hang? You ever see 'em at night? You know. You ever see 'em?'" Harry dropped his drink the last few inches onto the corner of the glass coffee table and drew back the curtains.

"No. Well, I'm not really looking, though—." Jackson was slowly getting the red face of a man who knows he's being made a fool of, but is trying to play along or at least keep up without acting like us.

"Hmm," Harry said, still looking out the window.

"Jackson's a PR professional for Bryant Spalding. He used to be a reporter, Will, if you're interested in trying to get that going again." Penny was trying to make this work or at least to keep us civil.

Suddenly I felt guilty for acting like an ass. "Really? What paper?"

"Well, the *Midtown Chronicle* for one. I did a few city papers, nothing really mainstream, though."

"Yeah, you worked for the Billings, right?" The Billings were one of Atlanta's wealthy families from back when Buckhead was just a bar with a deer head on the wall and Peachtree was a dirt road. The current patriarch served as dictator for a number of neighborhood papers. Harry knew this because he read everything he got his hands on and remembered every word. Jackson thought someone had finally recognized him from his work and was as loyal as a puppy to Harry until the end.

"Y-yeah. He's an ass, Ross, that is. Guy used to come in after being gone for three months and try to reinvent the wheel in the newsroom. He's notorious for it. That's partly why I left, aside from the hours. I don't miss the hours."

Nearly everyone in public relations graduated with an English or journalism major, got to a newspaper, wrote for three months, and then realized that Hemingway said he was a writer despite having worked for a newspaper, not because of it. The hours soon caught up with them, along with negligent paychecks, and they got swept away with the idea of writing releases and getting paid big cash. The payoff, of course, was if you could make it big and be a communications director or a media contact for a big company or a politician.

Then seven months down the road, call four in three hours from a forty-five-year-old woman who hired your firm to help publicize her bowl-a-thon turned your great idea into a bad one and you were back to square one.

"But, really, I know some people who could help you get a job."

"What? And leave the lucrative world of restaurant critic? Not on my watch, sister." By now Jackson knew Harry's game and played along and offered him another drink rather than taking offense.

Oren was silent and as Penny paced the room, she avoided his eyes and he hers. The fact that he was infatuated and that she had played along was painfully obvious, at least by now, to everyone in the room except for Jackson. Jackson was just excited to be playing host to people who were not raised inside of the perimeter and whose world, surprisingly, did not revolve around annual invites to the Swan House Ball, Junior League activities, and the Driving Club. He thought we were a novelty but he was the same to us and I thought it was great.

"Where are you from?" asked Harry.

"Well, actually, my parents live on West Paces Ferry," Jackson said. "We're real Atlanta." Any family with at least four generations could make that claim and, likewise, deny it to those without. "Next to the governor's mansion. Anyway, we're not Civil War vets." That would have been an extra feather in his hat for his "Old Atlanta" connections.

The wind whipped the trees into a frenzy outside the window and they swayed and groaned the way I remember trees groaning when I was a child. It was unseasonably cold, not at all what I'd expected from a Southern fall. To keep warm, Oren and I mixed martinis and sneered at Jackson's indulgent apartment.

We were drunk when we left and wore our revolutionary defiance like campaign buttons.

"You'll have to meet my parents sometime. I'd like them to see some of Penny's family."

"They might not like that." Penny was serious, but agreed to let me come if I behaved.

One night, Penny took me to meet the Rigsbeys. She was tiring of Jackson by then. He had turned into a starry-eyed lover and I asked Penny if she thought he was likely to turn gay after she broke his heart. She didn't answer.

We reached the Rigsbeys' at seven and I tapped on the backseat window of Jackson's car as the gate blocking the driveway slowly opened.

"That the governor's mansion?"

"Yeah."

"Is it nice?"

"I don't know. I've never been in it."

Alessandro, the Rigsbeys' part-time housekeeper, met us at the door and smiled and clasped Jackson's hand in his.

"Your parents are in the living room."

I looked at the paintings on the walls in the rooms leading to the living room and at the sculptures and vases and Jackson gave a tour the best he could, giving dates and artist names and what period the pieces came from.

"What were your parents' influences when they decorated?" I asked.

"We picked what looked good, dear. What matched." Mrs. Rigsbey stood at the entrance of the living room. Her gray pants fell evenly on her shoes and her jewelry shimmered in the light of the chandelier.

"You must be Will. So nice to meet you. I love your sister." She gave Penny a stiff hug and pressed her cheek against Jackson's and made a kissing noise.

"Hello, Will. Thad Rigsbey." Jackson's father stretched a fleshy hand toward mine.

We went into the living room where Mrs. Rigsbey walked me through, pointing out each piece of art and stopping to talk about the ones by painters I would recognize.

"I live for this stuff, you know. I truly do," she said.

"I don't know what I would do without art," I said. "Of course, I see most of mine in a gallery, but—."

"Tell me, Will, what do you think of the South so far? Being a Yankee."

The question was loaded, but I spun my way around the trees and the beaches and Charleston's beautiful homes. I said that, as a place, Atlanta differed from Maine in ways immeasurable. But thousands of miles of separation did nothing to change the social climate of a people.

"I think that as a whole, bunched together to hunt and gather, people never change. The small-town stigma that Southerners bathe in sort of vanishes here."

She nodded and smiled with her teeth. "Don't forget about the hospitality, now. I've been to New York City. Everyone is so rude and in such a hurry. You don't see that here, not on West Paces." Her makeup creased as her tightly stretched face pulled back into a smile. Charleston was gone and so was the Old South and the beauty of it, but there were Old Southerners in Atlanta like her that stayed true to their ideas and said it was the Yankees who ruined it. They blamed us for the traffic and the smog and the fast pace. They walled themselves in sculptured neighborhoods with huge and beautiful trees and fought the development and pushed it to poorer neighborhoods because they were already ruined anyway.

"What do you think of the governor's mansion?" I asked.

"I don't, really. There are plenty of fabulous houses here. Most of these houses are kept up on a regular basis. Except for the smaller ones, but those people are just here so they can say they live on West Paces. A lot of transplants, really."

"Mom." Jackson's face was red again.

"Oh Jacks, they know what I'm talking about. There are two types of Yankees. You two are the good kind."

The poverty of rural Georgian towns is staggering. I never knew it was as bad as it is in movies until Delia took Harry and me home with her for a weekend. She was going to see her parents. We were going to see the South.

Delia's car wove through flat east Georgia roads between Atlanta and Augusta where her parents enjoyed the pseudo-aristocratic lifestyle of the South's rich and famous.

Al Rothberg was determined to prove himself a Southern Baptist and not a Jew and he met us at the Confederate flag-draped lamppost next to the driveway.

"Well, hey y'all." He hugged Delia.

"Hey Daddy." Her accent thickened.

We spent the night talking about the northeast while Delia feigned ignorance. Al made a fortune selling the family land plot by plot to the same carpetbaggers he frowned on and made even more in the market. He had a new bass boat, a house three sizes too large, more cars than good sense and a membership to Augusta National.

"Hell, I'd rather pull bass from the water hazards than plunk a birdie, but I like to get out there."

After dinner we sat on the porch and smoked cigars. Delia's mom silently lit candles placed around the ledge.

"Hey baby."

"Mmm-hmm?"

"Could you bring us some bourbon and water?"

"Mmm-hmm." She walked inside and Al yelled after her.

"And not too much water!"

Delia stayed inside with her mother and drank sweet tea and spent an evening in the pious spirit of a good Baptist. Al leaned back in his chair on the porch and told us stories about fishing in the Gulf and of weekend hunting trips and eating pickled eggs, summer sausage, and potted meats.

"Have you lived here your whole life?" Harry asked.

"Harry, you always talk like that?"

"Uh, yeah."

"Hell, I'm just kidding you. Your accent is just different is all." He smiled. "No. I lived in South Georgia when I was a boy. In a small town." He laughed and took a sip of his drink. "Hell, things were a lot different then. Daddy didn't have much money and mama really did nothing but raise us and I bet that ain't easy. I had enough with just Delia." He smiled when he said her name.

"So, is it like you see in the movies? Being backwards and segregated, I mean?"

"Hell, you get right to it, don't you boy? Like a genuine Yankee." He drew his vowels out until they were pulled loose. "I like that. I'll tell you things have changed since I was growing up. It was different—hell, we were different. I was raised with a different mentality than Delia was."

"Like what?"

"Well—."

"I don't mean to pry. Let me know if I say too much, but—."

Al cut him off. "No, no, not at all." He finished his drink and walked into the kitchen to make more. He came out with more bourbon, no water this time, just ice and lime.

"When we were young, we didn't go to school with blacks and didn't talk to them and they didn't talk to us. I didn't really know why, that's just the way it was. I know black guys today—and I like 'em. Why didn't I like 'em when I was younger? Just was taught not to. My parents never said, 'Hate blacks,' but it was known they felt that way. We could tell. But I don't wanna be too hard on no one. People all over the world are hatin' each other and killin' each other. It's just we admitted it and said we were wrong and now everybody knows how it was."

"So, did anything happen?"

"You mean, was there violence?"

"I don't know. Whatever you saw."

"Yeah, some of our parents did things that were bad and some of my friends did."

"Does that still happen?"

"Depends on where you go. In some small towns, not much has changed. My brother still lives down there and he told me that his sheriff killed some blacks a while back and everyone knows it."

Harry jumped forward in his seat. "He's not in trouble? How does he get away with that?"

"People are too afraid to say a word. The bodies are buried in a dam down there and when it cracked he told the mayor that he'd pay a private contractor to patch it."

"They didn't drain it and they knew?"

"Yup."

"Why?"

"Nobody wants to get into all that. There's a lot of shit—" He looked over his shoulder to make sure his wife wasn't behind him. "There's a lot of shit that's been around for a long time. Nobody wants to get into all that."

"But the black people. Aren't they pissed?"

"There's not a lot of education down there—black or white. People don't know their rights." And again the vowels were long and soft like water-rounded wood.

"But all they have to do is go to the police," Harry protested.

"What police don't know the sheriff?"

"Why can't they go to the state police or FBI?"

"I don't think you understand. There's little education and less trust for the law. They think it's been wrong too many times. It ain't the South as much as it's the remoteness of some of the towns." Al looked at the surprise on our faces and smiled. "Welcome to the country, boys."

I woke just after seven to the sound of Al spinning the tires of his four-wheeler through the mud by the back pond. The bourbon had knocked me out, but I woke, washed my face, and walked downstairs. Harry was still snoring. Mrs. Rothberg was making biscuits and gravy. I poured a cup of coffee and sat next to her on a stool.

"He always gets up early when he drinks. To show me that he didn't have too much."

I sat silently as she continued.

"It's just that he's a member of our church and we don't drink. Not in the presence of God."

I choked on my coffee and she handed me a napkin.

"And you're always in the presence of God."

Later, Delia told me on the ride back that Southern Baptists think anyone who drinks must be an alcoholic and that her father didn't drink in front of his parents. She said they bypassed temperance and headed straight for avoidance. I asked if people follow the rules and she told me that her father was a deacon. I asked her why she drank. "I'm a Jew," she said.

Al was finished driving around by nine and came in to eat breakfast.

"Y'all comin' to the pig roast?"

"The what?" My Yankee was showing.

"Hell, boy, for that you *have* to come." Al laughed and finished breakfast. Mrs. Rothberg walked around and silently cleaned the kitchen.

We showered and dressed and Al came downstairs in khaki shorts, a white collared shirt, and tan flip-flops. The cool of the morning air was gone and the hot wetness of the afternoon came down and choked in our lungs and stuck to our arms. We all piled into Al's black Tahoe and he tore down the long gravel driveway and turned onto the street. In ten minutes we passed out of Augusta's affluent reach and were passing through the dense woods and open fields.

"Bet y'all ain't seen woods like this, huh? Hell, we get 200-pound deer all the time." Al looked back at me and smiled. I smiled too. My father is an expert woodsman and I saw bigger animals than that when I was a child.

"Actually Al, the Northeast is mountainous and rural. Hell," I emphasized that word, "I've helped skin 2,000-pound moose."

"Huh."

The Rothbergs, aside from real estate and stocks, ran a landscaping firm with branches throughout Georgia and South Carolina.

"I keep these people employed, ya know." Al swept his hand across the sprinkling of trailers as we passed them on the highway. "Helps me sleep at night to know it. Man, it's hot in here." He reached down and cranked up the air conditioner.

We passed trailer parks and two-house clearings in the woods and neighborhoods of seven or eight houses sitting in open fields with burnt-out grass. Furniture and toys were scattered on the lawns, which spread back from the street to the small houses without porches. Those without doors had plastic hanging in the doorway like the entrance of a freezer and others had screens. Children, dirty and thin, played on the lawns and some ran out of doorless houses and stopped as we passed. They were Al's kids.

Al's friend Anderson was hosting the pig roast and when we got to his house three men with balding heads and callused hands ran from the truck to the pit to the tables, slinging coleslaw and pouring sauce and turning the spigot. Al introduced us as friends of Delia's and once it was known that we were Yankees, we answered questions and listened to men with thick accents tell us that Yankees were "awright."

We drank beer from plastic cups filled from a keg and gnawed on the tough chunks of meat and made sandwiches from the tender ones.

"Guess this is a Catholic party," Harry said to Al while we waited in the long line at the keg.

"Nope. We're all Southern Baptist."

If Friday night was for cigars and bourbon, Saturday night was no different. But we dutifully woke at seven on Sunday and went to church, with Harry in a silent protest. We drank grape juice instead of wine and Mrs. Rothberg smiled as Al's face and neck glistened with sweat after the service. We ate dinner at two and said good-byes and thank yous and walked out to the car.

"Hey, uh, if y'all wanna come back and set out and have a few drinks, why, you just come on. I'm getting to like you Catholics." Al smiled and Mrs. Rothberg turned and went into the house.

§

The weather broke for good in November. When the cold settles on the Southeast it comes late and quiet and nobody really knows that it's coming until it arrives. So our first cold night hit like a hammer, but passed when the sun came up. Harry wrote less and less for the *Review*. I was never sober. We met at the café less frequently but enough to be regulars.

I left Penny's one morning and the air was fresh and cold and when I walked outside it bit my face and woke me up. I stood by the curb, my hands stinging and arms shivering and watched as the cars passed. Some of them skidded and slipped on the ice, but most drove slowly because they were frightened by the apocalyptic newscasts that urged anyone not rushing to the store to get bread and milk to remain at home. The exhaust flowed in thick white streams from the tailpipes and I could taste the bitterness of it in my mouth.

I met Harry at Delia's before nine and we had breakfast and went to the *Review* to discuss the December issue. November had been a success. Michelle was a hit and our indifference and negligence was overlooked as shortcomings always are in the face of absolute victory.

"Harry, I loved your piece about the House of Chan. Loved it." Michelle repeated her words and Harry called her a jackal, but in her eyes he loved her.

"It was almost too cold to come today, but I knew you all would be here." She dropped her Alaskan-style parka on a chair and rubbed her bare arms and shook her bare legs.

"Michelle, you're only wearing a sleeveless sweater and a skirt," Harry said.

"I know."

"Well, then you're just fuc—."

"Harry, loved the piece about the House of Chan." One of the salesman breezed through the lobby and patted Harry on the arm and probably saved his job.

When we were on the balcony Harry lit his cigarette and handed the matches to me.

"First of all, it wasn't a piece. It was a restaurant review!"

"Not so loud, man. She's gonna hear you."

"Oh, like I care? A piece? Will, come on."

"Last time I checked, hombre, this was the only thing paying your bills. Delia gonna let you stay for free?"

"Who said it would be for free?"

"You lie. You two? You lie."

"Maybe. You'll never know."

Michelle took the office to lunch. We ate at Hard Rock Café and watched old music videos and carried on useless conversations. I turned to one of the salesmen and asked him what he thought of the election.

"I don't really."

"What?"

"Don't think about it, don't care. I don't follow all that stuff." He sipped his Coke and poked the ice with his straw. "I don't know anything about that." He laughed and someone else agreed. In high school ignorance was high fashion. Some fads die hard.

"Don't you care what happens to you?"

"To me? Tell me one way my life will change." It was a good point and maybe I didn't follow it closely because I had to think about it for a minute.

"Environment. You, uh, you have a candidate who wants to drill the Alaskan reserves for oil. They have two totally different international policies and one of them could bring us to war."

"So how does that affect me? Either way, the world will keep going. So should I waste my time with that?"

"What *do* you do?"

"I don't know." They both laughed. "I make money. Meet girls. Got a nice ride."

"Your car sucks, dude." The other chimed in and they hit each other on the arms.

"So you aren't interested at all in the world?"

"No. Just don't care. But I watched Britney last night on TV." They laughed again and I turned away. If they weren't going to take my help, I wasn't going to give it.

We walked outside and tiny droplets of rain seeped from the sky and dripped off the buildings onto the awning and formed little streams that fell from the canvas in large drops. One splashed on my neck and I drew my shoulders back and winced, then pulled up my collar. Four or five people stood in the rain around a light pole stuck in the sidewalk next to the curb. They were staring down on the street. Harry tapped my arm.

"That's where that guy was killed yesterday."

"Who?"

"Don't know. Courier. He was hit by a car right there."

We walked to the pole and read the placards leaning against it that his friends and family left. The words were rain-smeared and blue ink ran down the page and pooled up on the sidewalk. Faded spots of dried red in the street marked where he had fallen. As we watched, a voice boomed from behind us.

"Brothers and sisters! We have an epidemic here today that we can no longer turn our backs on."

I turned my head and through dripping bangs saw a man holding a sign that read SAVE OUR SOULS. He was handing out cards.

"We can no longer turn our heads and think this doesn't affect us. That is reality. It's right there and it's reality." He pointed a wet arm in the direction of the dried red. "We gotta stop the cars from flying around here." People on the street passed him by and shook their heads when he offered them a card.

"This is the most dangerous city in America for pedestrians. This is your problem. You can no longer pretend it does not exist. This is reality." He tried to hand me a card, but I pushed past him.

At two the rain finally stopped falling and then the sun came out and burned off the clouds. I left the *Review* at three and walked down the empty streets to the café. When I got there Oren was sitting around and Penny was there with Jackson. Harry walked in just after I did.

"I have a gig tonight." Oren's face was pale and his eyes were dark. "At Flamingo's." Flamingo's was a Mexican restaurant with a huge porch and they always had bands playing. Oren once said he'd never play there. He said the place was low rent. "I need some cash and Josh—you've met my drummer before, right? He's getting really anxious to play again. You know he almost quit last week."

"I know, you told me." He had. Twice, but I didn't point that out.

"What do you do with all of your money, anyway?" Penny was clean now or at least pretty damn close and she was tired of Oren.

"What do you care?" He knew she knew. We all knew. "Besides, you can always use more cash." Oren rubbed his face and cleared his scratchy throat. Only this summer he was an artist who cared less for money than he did for Penny. Today, he rubbed a swollen nose with shaky hands and ordered another drink.

"So?" Harry sat down and banged his drink on the table. "Guess who finished his first draft?"

We celebrated the afternoon with drinks and after a few hours Penny said we should leave and go to the Highlands. I went to the bathroom and as I walked out, Oren walked in. Everyone knew that the drugs had gotten out of hand and some of them had a part in it, but only the two of us got in as far as we did. It became a dirty secret and we'd sneak off one at a time and only took them for fun.

At seven Oren was gone and Penny and Jackson went out for dinner. Harry gave his manuscript to Delia and came back over to get me.

"Let's go, we're gonna be late and they don't play for long anymore," Harry said.

"Do I need a coat?"

"It's cold outside. Not too bad, but—just come on. I don't even know why we're going, I bet he gets too hopped up to—." Harry stopped. I pretended not to hear him and put on my coat and rubbed my hand hard over my face several times.

But he was right. Oren played the first set and got sick in the bathroom before the second. The manager of Flamingo's leaned against the stall and yelled at Oren and swore if he did not get up now, he'd never play there again. But he couldn't and he didn't.

℘

I was glad when the cold finally came and the heat and the sweat were gone. The cool took the heaviness from the air and in its place was the sharp snap of freshness. Outside it was clean and clear and on a cold morning I heard that Oren was gone. His drummer kicked him out of the band and replaced him with a sober singer. Just like that, it was over. Penny stayed inside and played with her pencil but never really put it to the pad. I got breakfast and brought it back. Penny was still in bed.

"Did you sleep last night?" I asked through her bedroom door.

"No." Her voice was soft and broken.

I rested my forehead against the wood. "You OK?"

"Yeah. I just worry about him. He's bad, you know."

"I know. I brought food." I took the food into her room and we sat on her bed and ate egg sandwiches and drank coffee and talked about things that weren't so heavy. It was too early for heavy talk. She broke the truce around eleven.

"You know, I think I—."

"I know," I said.

"We were together only once. The first cold night. You and Harry were gone and Oren came over and we had drinks."

"You don't have to—."

"I know. We had drinks on the balcony and watched our breath and spilled wine down into the street. He told me about his girlfriend." Her eyes went to the floor and she smiled. "He was—just slow and quiet and he poured wine and touched my hand. It was warm inside and we swore we wouldn't tell. We just rolled on the bed and he ran his hands through my hair. Slow. Just slow. He didn't say anything. Not a word all night. I was drunk and so was he, but it was slow and the cold air felt so good. He left at eight and we never said a word." She got quiet for a second before looking at me. "What's he gonna do now, Will?"

"I don't know."

"Where'd he go?"

"I don't know."

We hardly talked about Oren after that. Penny stayed in her room the rest of the day and she hardly said anything for almost a week. Her best writing came during that time and when she wasn't smearing the ink on the page it was poetry.

Harry brought his memoirs to Penny's later that week and by then they were slowly turning into a novella. When I woke up, Penny and Delia were in the kitchen pouring coffee into wide, clay mugs and Harry was smoking a cigarette on the balcony.

"You want any of this, Will?"

"Yes. Thank you." It was the first thing that Penny and I said to each other in three days.

"I don't think that I can do this today, Harry. I really don't." Penny had been awake most of the week listening to old records and writing.

"So? Let's do something else then. Where do we go?"

We went to the Mexican restaurant we ate at our first day in Atlanta and it was like nothing had changed. We ate chips and drank margaritas and my face was warm and red by one. After a plate of chili rellenos and another pitcher of margaritas, we rode MARTA to Peachtree Street and walked through the afternoon crowds of white-collar workers and homeless squatters. Everyone was rushing around in leather shoes and wool-blend pants, shivering as they passed the buildings on their way to lunch.

"It feels weird to be wearing sneakers and jeans when you're around people in suits on their way to work," Harry said.

"They call that freedom." Penny had been part of that world before running away.

"Have you ever had a job, Harry?"

"Nope. Glad, too. I could be doing this." He pointed to someone our age. "Living like him."

"Oops. Watch out." We passed a homeless man as he staggered around the side of a mailbox and talked to his bags.

"That's where too much freedom lands you," Delia said.

"You're bitter because you work down here."

"Actually, Harry, I'm not. Come see me when you get done with all of this playing and need a job and you have to start at the bottom and nobody cares about your philosophy."

Harry looked at me and I shook my head and shrugged.

"Never happen. Thanks for the invite, though."

We walked into the shops by the capitol and tried on glasses and got sized for leather shoes with four-inch soles and purple jackets. A pawnshop across from the courthouse sold gold teeth next to watches and radios. Outside of the business district the crowd changed and looked as casual as we did. Some were students and some were old men who stared at us as we passed and some were younger men who pushed passed us without a glance. When we got bored we hopped on MARTA and rode back to Penny's. Delia sat next to a man who told her about the Bible and asked if she had been saved. She said she was a Jew, so he took out his book and showed her its finer points until we got off.

※

Margaritas never go quietly and as I walked through the frozen streets in the morning my head felt heavy and swollen. The sky was light blue at the top and blended into a white mesh of clouds and smog on the horizon and the long morning shadows blocked the sun from wiping the streets clean of frost. Thin layers of ice settled on puddles and crunched when I stepped in them.

I got to the *Review* at nine and put together something about the Mexican restaurant. It was all praise, although I warned that they never took reservations and adamantly refused to split the check whether your party was two or twenty.

"Michelle, I have a review. You wanna see it?" In the beginning, editorial phases moved slow enough to keep pace with the dead.

"No. Just go ahead and put it through. Who is it?"

"Mama Nutoro's."

"Do they advertise with us?"

"No."

"Hmm. OK. Thanks." Success had proven the process true and she decided it was no longer necessary to pine over whether a restaurant's ambience was cozy or warm. Penny hated when I used words like cozy because they told rather than showed and made the piece choppy and it was bad writing. Michelle handpicked cozy.

I was in the lobby talking to some of the sales guys when I heard the door open and slam shut over the tap of leather-soled black shoes on the hardwood floors. Harry grabbed my arm and tugged at it until I looked at him.

"Hey boss," he was half-laughing and the words came out in between breaths. "I got something. Wrote it just now. You're gonna love it."

We smoked a cigarette on the balcony and went into the cubby-sized office where Harry and I entered our reviews.

"I went to the second-floor cafeteria in the Georgia Trust building, you know? And so I went there to get the review, just a joke, but I was gonna do something just to laugh at and then I get the idea to do it for real."

"Well, what the hell is it?"

"It's in my notebook." He waved the small green notebook that he carried in his pocket. "Let me type it out. I'm gonna give it to Michelle. You'll see."

When he was done, Harry walked across the lobby and pushed the notebook into my hands. His breathing was excited and shallow and he kept his eyes on the floor and walked into Michelle's office and dropped the typed copy into the box. The chair in the workroom squeaked when I sat in it and I looked around to make sure that no one was watching and read the review.

> I hear the incessant flapping of mouths, some sucking on food—others reciting the clichéd catchphrases that epitomize priggish lives. A woman with freakishly elongated limbs, whose height has drawn crook-neck stares and half-guarded insults for a fool's eternity, briskly passes a woman as short as a stump and no less than equally wide.
>
> In a moment, a woman contemplating abortion brushes against an equally tormented woman as barren as the depths of the sea. All the while, a third sports a well-groomed Afro, eating a salad smothered in heavy dressing and washing it down with a diet soft drink.
>
> And men, oh the nondescript men coming from nondescript houses driving nondescript cars going to

nondescript jobs where they chatter indiscriminately. Men so obviously dressed by their wives, exerting with great deference the very essence of their self-proclaimed manhood.

Mixed and mingled, closed ears press tight to gripping conversation and faithful eyes hold fast on the legs of passing women.

This is the scene at the corporate cafeteria, where self-proclamation poses as the indemnifying lover of self-loathing. It is similar to the high school cafeteria in that it is awash with rumors and gossip and overindulgence, but conspicuously void of childhood aspirations and the centuries-old quest for the realization of one's own self.

I highly recommend the liverwurst sandwich with spicy mustard, red onions, and Swiss on a plain bagel. Enjoy.

When we got back to Penny's there was a message on the machine from Michelle. She wanted to see Harry immediately. He called.

"Hello? This is Harry, what's up? Yes. Yes. Uh, yeah I did. Mm hmm. Yeah. Twice, I think. No. Not at all. Great." He hung up the phone and sat on the couch.

"So what'd she say?"

"Asked if I really wrote that. Asked if I was serious. If I expected to get fired. How many other times I wrote bogus stuff. And then asked if I saw a problem."

"Wh—."

"Then she goes, 'You can consider yourself fired.' I said, 'Great' and hung up."

"What the hell are you gonna do now?"

"Not confuse art with making a living."

In late November, I picked Harry up at Delia's and turned Penny's car toward the highway. It was gray and cold and we didn't talk much above the radio. I stopped at a light and a car full of teens pulled up alongside of us. They dipped their heads rhythmically to a beat we couldn't hear.

On the highway, the rain that was falling in tiny drops began to hit the windshield harder and faster. The drops smacked into the glass in clusters like raspberries. I turned on the wipers and they were gone. We drove outside of the perimeter and passed through the suburbs of Cobb and Norcross and Alpharetta where most of the people working downtown live.

"No way in hell I'd live out here and fight through all of this traffic every day."

"Harry, there's no traffic. Not today."

"Well, no. Not today. It's Sunday, but tomorrow, when they all go back to work—look out."

He talked about the standstills and the accidents and the fatalities and the heat and fumes coming off the road in the summer. But it wasn't the summer and none of those things were on the road. It was Sunday and all I felt was the tightening of my stomach that comes from years of habit. I was convinced, as a child, that when I was out of school and had no undone homework to face up to and when the trivial ins and outs of adolescent politics were gone, I would love Sundays as I loved Saturdays. That turned out to be no more true than my early belief that when I shut off my TV a disappointed production crew called it a day.

Harry talked about the disadvantages and boredom of suburban life and laughed at his jokes and insight and I faced Monday morning. And for no better reason than it was Sunday. I had left home and gone to Pennsylvania, traveled south and landed in Charleston and all this I had done alone. But now, on a Sunday, sitting next to a close friend who was on a roll, I felt more alone than I had in months.

We passed the near towns and the radio lost reception and turned to static when we slipped off of I-85 and onto I-985. Harry flipped the dial with no luck.

"Forget it." He switched the radio off and we listened to the tires sloshing through the rain and the tick tock of the wipers across the windshield.

I turned the car off the highway and onto a two-lane road that coiled around the mountain. The engine whined as we went down the steep hills and grew louder when we went back up. The trees grew close to the roadside. I looked out at the pines. Their trunks were bare except for the thin branches and the nubs of the ones that had already broken off. At the tops they unfolded like tall green umbrellas, blocking the dead needles on the ground from the sun. The other trees, thin and spindly, had lost their leaves and looked gray and cold against the white sky. Kudzu lined the ground like a fake green lawn and shined from the rain.

The brakes squeaked when I pulled the car, vibrating slightly, to a stop at a red light. The rain fell lightly on the windshield now and the wipers squealed as they pulled along their arch. The light was red and there were no other cars. And we sat alone, stopped at the light, listening to the wipers drag across the glass.

"I think we can turn to the right here." Harry checked the directions and pointed to the right.

"You sure? I thought we were supposed to go left."

"I did too. But I see now it's right. I say go right."

I turned the car and the rain began to hit the window hard again and the wind smeared it. The wipers glided along noiselessly. I made another right onto a small street with a wooded median and a large wooden sign that opened into a new development. The houses were sparse—one or two at a clip, then more empty lots, then more houses. The grass was new and light green or it was brown and dead and you could see where it had been rolled down. Blocks of wood with numbers spray-painted on them marked the end of one lot and the beginning of another. The few houses already standing were not built proportionately and gobbled up most of the lawn, allowing prying eyes to see from one window to the next.

Charles Fortier, a book agent from Florida, lived in lot 42, across the street from the builder's trailer. I kicked mud from my feet as I stepped off the lawn and stood on the concrete porch while Harry rang the doorbell.

"Harry, nice to see you. You found it OK?"

"Not a problem."

Charles looked at me from the corner of his eye. His shirt was open and his hair looked like he used too much gel.

"Charlie. Charlie Fortier."

"Will."

"Will gave me a ride. I have no car and no license."

"Hmm. OK. It's just we have a lot to do and the office is small." He let us in and offered me a seat at the kitchen table before disappearing with Harry into a bathroom-sized office.

When the door closed behind them, I walked around the house and looked at pictures. I passed a hutch full of china and crystal and silverware that shook and rattled like a circus wagon when I walked by. Charlie had an old grandfather clock with the chains and the grinding gears that reminded me of one my grandparents had. When I was little I used to lie on the couch and fall asleep to the sound of the ticking and my grandmother talking in the background.

A sudden bang jerked me from my thoughts.

Mrs. Charlie kicked the front door open and slammed it shut behind her. As she walked through the foyer into the kitchen, I jumped and tried to get as far out of the living room as possible before she saw me. I made it less than halfway.

"Who are you?"

"Uh, Will. Your husband is meeting with my friend. About a book."

"Oh." Her voice got flat when I said it. She looked at me with full eyes and evenly, nothing like Charlie had. "Come and sit in the kitchen."

She threw her bags on the counter and opened a drawer next to the phone.

"This damn drawer has so much crap in it." She pulled out a wooden spoon and a pair of scissors, salad tongs, and a lighter. "Damn it." She grabbed a white book from underneath utensils and pictures and pulled it out. Another pair of scissors fell to the floor. I sat at the table, staring out the window and playing with my hands while she flipped through the book. I held my breath and tried to let it out slowly to keep from making noise while she looked. She grabbed the phone and fumbled it off the hook and started punching numbers. Tapping her fingers wildly on the counter, she looked up at me. I froze. I wiggled my toes. I wished Harry had a damn license. My breathing was getting loud again.

"Judy. This is Anne Fortier. How are you? That's nice. I have a problem. Yes." She glared at me and then back at the pages in her white book.

"Judy, when we moved in you told me that this subdivision had rules. No broken-down cars, no flamingos in the yard, everyone must turn on their lights between eight and nine during Christmas so we can drive around to see them. Well, we have a problem. Yes. Who moved into 1781? On Briar. Sure, I can wait." She bit at her lips and I looked back at my hands.

"OK, the Styles? Well, did you know that they have painted their door pink? Yes and—." She popped her head up and caught me looking. I could feel my skin getting hot and the tiny drops of sweat on my neck. I moved my hands. She shuffled her feet.

"And they haven't cut their lawn once I bet. Now, most of us haven't, but that's because we have no goddamn grass, Judy. Now, this shit isn't proper. No. No. I'm not yelling at you. I just want our rules committee to put a little bite in their bark. We have the rules, we need to enforce them."

Anne hung up the phone. She closed her white book. She crammed the items back in the drawer and forced it shut.

"Where are you from, Will?" she asked, turning from the drawer and fixing her hair.

"Maine."

"Huh." She crossed her arms and looked out the window.

※

After Harry came out of the office, we walked out the door and got into the car and I pulled out of the driveway almost before I started the engine.

"This is a long way out. You can drive yourself next time or ride a bicycle."

"There won't be a next time."

"Huh?"

"He wanted nothing to do with it."

"Why?" His writing was good and it was fresh. I wish I could have written what he wrote.

"It's new. They won't take chances on something new."

We drove back to the city in silence but I felt less lonely than I had on the way out. The temperature dropped steadily as we drove south on 85. It got so cold that the car stiffened and we hit the potholes with a dull thud and slid and bounced around on the frozen vinyl seats.

We got off at Courtland and drove through the city. Cold wind, funneled by the buildings and drawn through the alleys, whipped through the streets, pushing leaves and papers into swirling fits of graceful aggression. Before we reached Penny's the temperature had dropped again and the gray clouds that had hung over the city all afternoon dropped big flakes of new white snow. The wind was still blowing and the flakes flew at a slanted pace and some spun in circles and they stuck to the sides of buildings as much as they did to the street. In less than an hour, a blanket of snow had dipped down and sat on Atlanta. Penny was on the porch when we pulled up to the curb.

"God, it's been so long since I've seen snow." Penny lived in El Paso before Atlanta and the heat had barely allowed rain. "Let's walk to the train tonight."

We walked to Delia's who pulled on a long wool coat and gloves and a hat.

"I haven't seen anything like this since New York." She tied a scarf around her neck and looked at Harry who agreed.

When we were young Penny used to drag me out in the snow and she'd run around the yard with our dog all afternoon. When we were older we walked through the woods and she used to whisper to match the silence of the snowfall.

"Man, you remember when we used to walk around at night?" she asked. "All you could smell was the burning wood in fireplaces." She stuck her hands in her pockets. "It gets quiet in the snow. Even now." The wind whistled in our ears and Harry and Delia chattered about life in the city. "But at night. In the woods. When you can hear the flakes falling. It's rhythmic."

I turned back to the snow and listened for the flakes. Penny blew into her hands, rubbed her red ears and nudged me with her shoulder.

"Something's changed, Will. I don't know what it is, but something's changed."

"I know."

We met Jackson for dinner and then walked to the café, but it was shut down.

"You've gotta be shitting me," Harry said.

Black curtains hung in the windows suspended by rods and through tiny folds in the material we could see lights and tables in the room.

"I think it's gonna be a dance club. Doesn't it look like a dance club?" Delia asked.

"Is that all you think about?" Harry and Delia were beyond the formal pleasantries of a friendly relationship and of other relationships as well.

"Well, let's go back by my place. I know a bar there. It's great."

We went back to Penny's to get Jackson's BMW convertible and sat on top of each other's laps all the way to Midtown.

"OK, someone has their hand somewhere they shouldn't."

"Oh shut up, Delia, at least it's just someone's hand," said Harry.

"Will you two shut up already?" Penny yelled.

"Easy for you to say when you don't have a seatbelt going up your—."

"Harry! You'll be OK." Penny looked at Jackson with heavy eyes. "I feel like my mother. Only I don't have Valium."

The ride to Jackson's apartment should have taken ten minutes, maybe less. But it took more than thirty and would have taken longer without the shortcuts. Understandably, Southerners aren't accustomed to snow and fall into a general state of hysteria when they have to drive in it. But the panic we saw on the streets could only have meant that discretion and common sense had been shipped out of town on the same train. Four-door SUVs skidded sporadically as their soccer mom drivers from encroaching suburbs panicked while transporting their one-child cargo in a 2,500-pound truck. Cars braked hard on ice and into turns, swerved sharply on frozen overpasses and anyone not cruising by at seventy-five meandered along at a cool thirty miles per hour.

The traffic caught us on Peachtree and got worse when we skidded onto the highway and remained steady through the back roads and cut-throughs to Midtown.

"OK, OK. My ass is numb. I want everyone to know that my ass is numb," Harry announced.

"Harry, why are you the only one complaining?"

Jackson rubbed his hand on the windows to clear the fog and eased the car into his space and shut off the engine. Harry yelled for him to hurry up and open the door.

"Let me out of here. Oh, that's better." He stretched his arms toward the sky and leaned his face back and let the snow fall on it. "Oh! My foot's asleep. It's asleep. Can't even walk on it. Jackson! Jackson carry me inside!"

Two days before Thanksgiving, Harry was gone. Delia called Penny's at nine and said that she hadn't seen him since the day before. Had we seen him? I told her we hadn't.

I went to the Schroeder building and talked to Michelle. He hadn't been there since the day he wrote his last review. She said she was too mad to care. Then, as I was leaving she said, "Will, if you find him, give me a call."

"OK." I walked back down the stairs and out into the district and walked past the tables where we ate lunch and looked in the windows of his favorite restaurant.

I rode MARTA back to Penny's and she was awake when I walked inside.

"You want some coffee?"

"Yeah." I took off my sweater and laid it across the back of the chair.

"Where do you think he went?"

"I really don't know. Knowing him, he went out last night and met someone and just didn't come home."

"A girl?"

"Could be. Maybe he just met some people that he liked and partied with them and didn't feel like leaving at four in the morning."

"You think he's with a girl?"

"I just told you I don't know. Besides, what if he is?"

"Well, he's with Delia and—."

"And what? Are they even really together?"

"It's not right."

"He can do what he wants. He's a big boy. Anyway, she doesn't own him." My voice got louder and I added quickly, "She knew that."

"That's not how he acted."

"What's your problem? I don't care what he does. He can do whatever he damn well feels like."

"It's not right and you guys have to give up this gypsy mentality and grow up!"

"Who the hell are you to say that? You're no better." My face felt red and tiny drops of spit were collecting at the corners of my mouth.

"Grow up. It's time to grow up."

"Don't tell me to grow up. I'm not the one being childish."

"Really? What about all that shit with you and Oren? That wasn't childish?"

"Yeah. Yeah Penny. What about Oren?"

She opened her mouth and then closed it slowly. Her eyes sank to the floor and she let her hands fall to her sides. "I don't know."

"There's no difference."

"But I know it doesn't work."

"Not for you. Not entirely."

"I'm not happy, Will." She brushed her hands through her hair and reached for a pack of cigarettes and lit one. When she put down the lighter I lit one and threw the lighter back on the table. She smoked the cigarette and played with her fingers before turning to me again. "I'm not happy."

"I know."

"No. You don't."

"What are you gonna do?"

"I'm going home. I didn't leave right." She sighed. "I wanna change that."

"I'm not going there. I'm never going."

"I know." She crushed her cigarette out and walked into her room and shut the door.

I looked for Harry for two more days. I called people we knew in Atlanta and called everyone from Charleston. Jack and Jay were gone and so was Cal, but Alex was there and he hadn't heard from Harry but would call if he did. At the end of the second day I called Harry's parents in Queens. His mother answered the phone and when I asked her if she knew where he was she handed him the phone and he came on and said, "Hey boss."

"What are you doing?"

"Eating."

"Damn." I put my hand on the table and sighed.

"What?"

"I was beginning to think that you were dead."

"Nope."

"Well, what are you doing?"

"I had to get out of there. You know, same old thing all the time, same people. The South. It was too much. Had to get back on the block."

"So you coming back?"

"No. Staying here. Got a job here. Gonna stay and save some money."

"You *what*? Well, then what?"

"Don't know. Probably stay here and work, though."

"So, you're just going back? What about writing? I can't believe you would just leave." I thought about that for a second and realized that it signified a change in me and a change in him, but it was bigger in him.

"We'll see," he said, quickly adding, "so how long are you gonna stay? You gonna get a job or you gonna bum around forever?"

"I don't know."

We talked for ten minutes before Harry got bored and rushed off the phone. I couldn't believe he just left and went home to get a job. Before we got off the phone Harry said he needed to do something and that he didn't want to be around anyone for a while. I asked him about doing what he loved and following his dream.

"Gotta pay the bills, boss."

I wish I could say when Harry left it didn't change things much but it did. Oren exploded and Harry just packed up and I was left with whatever I could sort out of what happened. So I got drunk. In the North it's a liquor store but down in the South it's a package store. I bought a couple limes, some ice, and a bottle of vodka. I didn't have the money for the good kind we drank when everything was great in Charleston. I only had a few dollars and I was in Atlanta. So I paid eight bucks for a half-gallon. Almost everybody I knew in the South drank bourbon in the hot sun but it never worked for me. So I drank vodka and even if it wasn't bourbon, being drunk reminded me of them.

Penny had old tumblers in her kitchen. I grabbed one, filled it with ice, mashed a half a lime into pulp, and mixed it in a glass with vodka. There was the bitter taste of the lime and the burning in my throat from the vodka. The first glass was gone before I really even thought about it. The second had less ice and more vodka and by the third I was wishing Oren was there because you can really get high when you've got this much alcohol to wash your drugs down with.

I'm not sure if we peaked too early again like Harry said. Maybe Oren did and Harry just got afraid of peaking at all because if you made it there was nowhere to go but down. That's why Delia never wrote. She never said it, but she stalled a hundred pages into her book and every time she added more she deleted something else. Like Ulysses' wife with the blanket. Only Delia just couldn't face herself if she finished and it wasn't good. And that was the change in Harry. Change from living his life to forcing himself into someone else's. The fact that I knew it maybe meant I was seeing things differently.

But I figured I was just thinking drunk because why would Harry do that? He was good. Who would do that if they were so good? You don't waste talent. Doesn't make sense. Just like I wasn't making sense, down past the middle of that label and really getting blind drunk on Penny's balcony.

And it doesn't make sense now and I wonder why I did it but at the time there was nothing to do but get in Penny's car and head downtown. So I grabbed her keys and walked outside. I can't remember walking down the steps or turning the car on but I was flying down the road before I realized I was driving. Right turns, left turns. Changing lanes and stopping at lights. Even not stopping at lights. It was mid-afternoon on a Saturday. People were out all over and I sped down the tiny stretch of I-20 between East Atlanta and downtown.

In Charleston, Jack always drove home drunk. We'd leave the beach one big drunken ball of sandy, half-employed nothing and it was just a party all the way back. When we'd get to Harry's we'd start all over again. But now I was alone. Just me in a car, vodka still burning the back of my throat. My head hot and starting to spin from trying to focus on the roads with the afternoon sun coming down blinding yellow in my face. Alone with nobody here. And still drunk.

It could've just been that I was thinking too hard and didn't see the turn, but the road moved out from under me and I skidded across a grassy lot and wedged Penny's car fifteen feet into a row of bushes somewhere near Freedom Parkway. It all just happened so slowly and gently it seemed like it never happened and I got out and walked away.

But when I got to Ponce there was Zesto's and all the memories and then the realization that it was all over. I was alone and drunk on the side of the road.

I don't know what I said to her, but I called Penny collect from a pay phone and she rode the train down to get the car out of the bushes and drive me home. She barely said anything and that would have made me feel even worse if I hadn't passed out.

At nine, I woke up in the car. Shivering with my head pounding and my stomach turning into knots. I walked inside, threw up in the bathroom, and went to bed. Penny woke me up at eight in the morning and didn't want to talk about it, not even to let me apologize. So it faded like my hangover and we spent the day sitting on the couch watching television and smoking cigarettes.

Now that it was over, there was nothing for me to do except keep going like I was. Either that or leave. So the next day I left Penny's and rode MARTA to the *Review* and told Michelle that I was leaving. She smiled and said she had expected it. There were other writers in the lobby and I had not seen them before, but they were there now and the *Review* was a success.

Penny met me at the door when I got back and smiled and said she was going to cancel her lease and drive to Maine. I asked what she was going to do and she said she had no idea but she wanted to go home.

She half-smiled and said, "I'm sorry I told you to grow up."

I didn't answer, but just looked at her. She got uncomfortable and looked out the window.

"The sun's out," she said.

"But it's cold."

She turned to me and took a deep breath.

"You know, I guess it's not about growing up. But it's not about not growing up." She sat down across from me at the table. "Will, I don't know anything. But I've learned that you have to find what makes you happy and do it. You can't run away."

"I know."

"Do you really think so? I know Oren didn't. He spent so much time running he never stopped to see he'd already gotten where he was going."

"Well, then maybe Harry realized something when he went back home. I mean, maybe Delia was right and we'll all have to settle down. So maybe he just went and did it and now maybe I should too."

She shook her head in disbelief. "You haven't learned shit."

"What?"

"Will, you're still a baby all wrapped up in this..." She waved her hands in front of me. "This seriousness. You can't even see straight you're so confused." She lit another cigarette.

"Harry made the biggest damn mistake of any of you." She paused and scuffed her foot on the floor. "He settled."

"How do you figure?"

"Because he won't see it until it's too late. Why the hell do you think Oren left? He could see it. He knew what he did. But Harry?" She laughed and blew smoke out of her mouth straight up into the air. "He thinks he's *on* the right path. He thinks because one person rejected him it means he can't do it. Poor Harry won't realize he gave up too soon until his life's gone by and there's nothing left for him to do except sit down and figure out what that emptiness is."

I looked down at the table and nodded my head. She got quiet and I pulled a cigarette out of her pack and lit it.

"So now what?"

"Now there's just you, Will. *Do* something."

"Like what?"

"I can't tell you that. You have to find your own gold."

"Well, what are you gonna do?"

"I think I'm done for now. I don't know who I am really." She'd been through too much for someone so young, but there was a light in her eyes that I couldn't remember ever seeing. "I don't know what I have, I just know I wanna start over. The right way."

"You're really going home?"

"Yeah."

We sat at the table for a minute, blue smoke from the cigarettes making the air hot and stuffy.

"What about you, Will?"

"I'm not sure." I laughed out a mouthful of smoke.

Penny left the next morning. Packed her stuff all night. She gave me a hundred bucks for bus money and was gone. And so I was alone in Atlanta. No friends and no place to go. I wasted the whole day. Alone and sober. At sunset I was still downtown. To the east the sky was dark. To the west, gold. I ate at the House of

Chan that night—AJ, party of one. It was cold and I waited next to the space heater. I drank tea and only one Tsingtao and had Mongolian Beef. I was wondering what the hell I was going to do next and watching the owner. He was trying to speak English and smiling all over, his eyes lighting up at each customer. Running his restaurant like there was nothing else. I started laughing and almost spit up my Tsingtao.

When the owner came over to say hello I told him that I was leaving. Going to California to find Sal and maybe write a little. He nodded happily, but he could never really understand English and he just smiled and walked away.